SHADOW'S TORMENT

TRISH HEINRICH

FIRST EDITION
ISBN:
ISBN-13: 978-1-7331880-3-6

Edited by Maria D'Marco and Dan Heinrich
Cover art & design by Todd Downing

WWW.TRISHHEINRICH.COM
Published by Beautiful Fire
706 Hull Ave, Port Orchard WA 98366 USA

simple as hair could be political or a part of the narrative of racism in our country, but it very much is. I did not go into this extensively, though I think it influenced certain parts of this book.

I hope I have respectfully portrayed this part of African-American culture.

Thank you for reading this little note. I hope you enjoy Shadow Dreams!

WINTER-1961

CHAPTER ONE

The dream started the same as it had most nights for the past year.

He and his two best friends, Alice and Lionel, stood on a rooftop, smoke spewing from windows below, enveloping them in a putrid cloud. They'd fought valiantly against Phantasm and the terrified men and women she'd created. But they'd lost.

Lost Park Side to carnage and flame.

Lost the chance to take down Phantasm.

Lost the chance to cure Lionel from the poison that was eating away at his tenuous control over his temper.

Now, here they were, trying to get off the roof before the flames or crazed people killed them.

In the dream, Marco looked around the roof top, sweat running down his chest and face. Screams echoed around them, the boom of explosions rocked the ground. Then, in the midst of this chaos, the world turned as silent as a graveyard. Dense smoke swirled, revealing a child with red hair kneeling on the rooftop. After a moment of staring at the kid, Marco realized he was playing marbles.

"This didn't happen," Marco whispered in the dream, his voice echoing.

He wanted to see who the boy was, to get closer, to find out why this child was in this dream. As if wishing could made it happen, Marco was right next to the boy in a blink.

The boy's face was broad, almost chubby. With a stubby finger, he flicked a marble into a circle drawn in the ashen dust covering the rooftop. The sharp clink of one marble hitting another was the only sound.

"Who are you?" Marco asked.

"Gone," the boy answered.

"What is?"

"I am. But you must find me."

"I don't…You weren't here."

"No," the boy answered.

An explosion rocked the building, and just like that, Marco was back at the edge of the roof top, watching Alice fall onto the fire escape. His heart lurched and his voice died in silent warning.

He knew what came next. What always came next. And, just like that day, he wouldn't be able to stop it.

Alice stared up at him from the rickety fire escape, her blue eyes full of fear.

Another explosion and the fire escape began to break away from the building. Lionel grabbed the bars and held it up, but as always, he wouldn't be able to for long.

Now Marco's screamed down to Alice, begging her to reach for him, in spite of her injuries. As she tried, her screams of pain and fear pierced through the other noises, striking Marco's very soul.

Another explosion, this one louder, larger, more devastating.

Reaching over the rooftop's edge, Marco was desperate to make his fingers longer, to somehow grab her as she fell into the smoke below. Her screams echoed around him, building to an excruciating crescendo.

And in the middle of it all, a new voice was added.

"Find me!" screamed the little boy. "Find me!"

———

Marco shot straight up from under the heavy blanket, his lanky body drenched in sweat, a scream dying on his lips.

At first, he wasn't sure where the hell he was, then it all hit him and he started to shiver. Not from the cold, though his sparse bedroom was chilly. No, he could be bundled in layers of fur and wool and he'd still shiver. At least until he could calm his nerves, remind himself that Alice was alright, that he was safe. After a few minutes, his body stilled and he ran a hand through his dark hair.

At least I've stopped throwing up from the dreams...

His stomach gave an unpleasant lurch and Marco rolled quickly from his bed, padded to the bathroom sink, and turned the water on full blast. The bright naked bulb overhead cast sharp shadows and made him squint. The water he flung at his face was so cold it made his long fingers hurt after a few moments.

He braced his hands on either side of the cracked sink, the chipped floor tiles under his thin socks cold as ice. Marco stared at the water gushing from the faucet and sighed, trying desperately to shake the dream. Screams still echoed in his mind. He closed his eyes and instantly saw Alice falling again.

Shoving his cupped hands into the stream of icy water, he doused his face, gasping at the cold. His eyes were now wide open, and he thought of the little red-haired boy.

"Who was that?"

He'd been haunted by that day at Park Side for over a year. But now, with this new addition to his dreams, Marco felt something was lurking in the back of his mind. Something his instincts told him should be remembered, but wasn't.

The more he tried to pin down how the boy had looked, and if he'd seen the child before, the more the memories slipped away, until Marco grunted in frustration and dried his face with a thin towel.

"I better change, it's...oh crap!" he said, looking at his wrist watch.

He'd fallen asleep just after lunch, hoping for a short nap and hadn't bothered to set an alarm. Now it was half past five and he was late for his nightly appointment with the man who was making Lionel's cure.

He charged into his room, shedding his sweat-soaked clothes on the way. Sleeping fully clothed had become a habit of his recently, when late night hours necessitated he get sleep whenever and however possible.

Slipping on a fresh shirt and pants, Marco ran to his closet, which he had converted into a make-shift dark room, and examined the images he had hung up to dry earlier that day.

Dirty pictures were an implied part of a private investigator's job, but not something Marco ever thought he'd face. Now, here he was in a cramped closet, hating himself just a little bit more than usual. But money was money, and he had to eat, right?

He quickly scanned the half dozen photos before him, relieved they were decent enough, though maybe not exactly what his client, Mr. Banks, wanted.

"Gotta draw the line somewhere..."

In two steps he was stuffing his feet into his shoes, which sat by the bed. The springs under the thin mattress creaked as he sat down. He noticed a few books had fallen from the bedside table and more than a few scary looking dust bunnies. He'd have to clean later this week, if he remembered.

As he stood and smoothed the thin blanket on the bed, something crunched under his foot. Frowning, he picked up the now-cracked picture frame that usually sat by the bed. He indulged in a long look at the beautiful woman in the picture.

Alice smiled at him, her eyes gleaming, curls an adorable mess around her face. He could almost hear her laughter.

The harsh honk of a car outside and a drunk yelling below Marco's window jolted him out of his thoughts. He set the frame with care on the bedside table and got moving, if he was late…

"Shit, where's my…oh…there it is…" He grabbed his wallet and keys from the wobbly dresser that was also covered in neatly stacked books.

He raced out of the bedroom, the only place that Marco could say was his living space, and stopped in the living room of the tiny apartment that acted as his Private Investigator office. A large old desk that had seen better days sat in the middle of the room, neat piles of paper and a cup of pencils sitting on top. But what Marco needed was tucked safe in the locked lower drawer. The lock stuck and he had to jiggle the key several times before it gave and he could grab a slip of paper. He shoved it into his trench coat, and stowed his grappling gun into his shoulder holster.

Though he'd left behind the hero persona of Shadow Master in Jet City, Marco had begun to realize that there were times when the ability to quickly climb to the top of a fire escape was an invaluable asset. Especially when someone was chasing you with a knife.

"Speaking of…"

He patted his chest and swore.

He hadn't put on the tattered reinforced shirt and vest

from his Shadow suit under his shirt, something that had saved his life more than once while on a job.

Once he'd slipped it on and rebuttoned his shirt, Marco walked into the small space to the left of his office that was laughably called a kitchen, and turned the radiator off. He wondered if he had time to eat, or if he even had any food in the small, groaning ice box. A glance at his watch told him he'd have to deal with an empty stomach for another few hours.

It's fine. After tonight, everything will be different anyway, and I'll…

He didn't complete his thought, he never could. He'd come close many times to finishing what he came to Metro City to do, but could never see what came after. He knew he'd never go back to Jet City, at least not to stay. There was nothing for him there.

Marco shook his head and forced himself to focus on the task at hand. He threw on his trench coat, gloves and a wool scarf that made his neck itch. With one last glance at his watch, Marco darted out of his apartment, making sure all three locks were secure and ran down the rickety steps.

The cold in Metro City still shocked him. Instead of the wet chill that he was used to in Jet City, this was a dry, knife-like cold that pierced his insides in seconds. Especially when the sun went down and the sky was clear like it was now. He looked up and wished he could see stars , but there was just enough light from the apartments and sparse street lamps that he could barely make out the very brightest ones.

At least the wind has died down. Turning the collar of his trench coat up, he walked with long, quick strides down the litter-strewn sidewalk.

His apartment building was at the very center of the neighborhood known as the Devil's Own, a haven for people who wanted to do their illegal activities in the relative peace of anonymity. This made it easy for Marco to pursue his activities without being noticed.

It did, however, have the disadvantage of making it hard to get clients. Marco often met with those that wanted his services at a local diner at a junction point of the Devil's Own and the more respectable neighborhood that butted up against it. Most only knew his phone number and Marco didn't mind keeping it that way.

As he put on more speed, Marco heard muffled cries from an alley and stopped. His powers itched under his skin, and he let himself reach out, just a little. A hint of fear, tangy and bitter, came to him, but more than that was a greedy lust and a strong arousal.

He knew several of the prostitutes and pimps that worked the Devil's Own. Some of them had even hired him on occasion to track down an aggressive John or a girl who'd gone missing. What he was sensing now was one of these women with a client, not an assault.

With effort, Marco shoved the remnants of the emotions away and continued on. It took several minutes for the after taste of the feelings to fade, during which time he managed to get into an even more dangerous part of the neighborhood than the area he lived in.

I could go around but that would take too much time and I'm already late to meet Dr. Brennan.

He could feel the emotions from dark alleys and doorways like an oily caress on his mind. So much hate and fear, so much greed and lust. It coated his mind and made him feel drunk.

Damn it! I don't have time for this!

It was usually easier to shut everything out, but it had

been weeks since he'd let his shadows out, and when it had been that long, controlling is powers became difficult.

The world was starting to go silvery gray, a sign that his shadows were going to come out whether he liked it or not. He stumbled down an alley let his powers have some freedom. As the shadows twisted out of his body, Marco sighed with relief. The emotions he felt from the people around him lessened, slowly, like an infection being drawn from a wound. He opened his eyes after several minutes, and the world had changed fully now into the silver-gray landscape of his powers. The shadows were dense and excited, crawling over him and the slimy pavement like delighted children too long confined.

Before he could stop them, the shadows sought out the source of these feelings. Marco could see the closest two people's minds, like rickety houses with rotting foundations.

The shadows got as close as the front door of their minds before Marco jerked on the tether he'd learned to keep on them. It was like reining in a dozen large dogs at once, and he grit his teeth against the strain on his own mind.

Slowly, he eased the shadows away from the houses that held those people's minds and forced them back to him. The world returned to its normal, drab colors as the shadows retreated completely inside Marco. He could still feel the aftertaste of emotion on his mind and cringed. Imagining his own mind like a house, he pictured himself taking a gleaming broom and sweeping the refuse of those feelings out the front door. It didn't get rid of them completely, but it definitely helped.

Seeing peoples' minds like houses was a trick he'd learned from...

Marco frowned.

He couldn't exactly remember how he'd learned that

particular trick, though he knew it had been just after his mother had died.

I must've read it. Doesn't matter.

He took a deep breath and pushed away from the alley's slimy brick wall.

In a few blocks, sweat drying on his chilled body and hunger grinding a hole in his gut, Marco was able to hail a cab. It smelled like old cigars, sausages and feet but he didn't care. Restraining his powers had sapped his energy and he was grateful for a safe place to rest.

"Where to pal?" the cabbie asked.

Marco gave him the address and ignored the raised eyebrow of the driver.

When the car pulled away from the curb, he closed his eyes and tried to get in the right head space for the night ahead.

CHAPTER TWO

Marco and Lionel had been in the city just a few months when Lionel's temper was unleashed at a local bar. Marco had tried to rein him in, and Lionel had thrown him across the room, breaking Marco's arm and giving him a nasty concussion.

That had been the breaking point for Lionel.

Once he knew Marco was going to be alright, he took off. A few weeks later Marco received a telegram from Lionel stating that he was in Europe and to not go looking for him. After that, Marco was more determined than ever to find the poison's cure.

He had decided to approach each scientist on the list they'd come up with, until he found the one that could reverse the effects of the poison. But each man either ran from him, were murdered or simply disappeared when Marco tried to ask for their help. As each name was crossed off, he became increasingly desperate. Finally, he found the last man on the list, a Dr. Brennan, who was posing as a pediatrician and lived in the Park Lane neighborhood of Metro City.

When Marco had approached Brennan, the man soiled himself in abject terror, convinced Marco was there to kill him.

"I never saw their faces at the labs, only...only intermediaries! I swear it. I won't tell anyone what I did, you don't have to get rid of me!" Dr. Brennan had pleaded.

"I'm not here to kill you," Marco had said. "I need your help."

It took most of the night to get the terrified man to help Marco. In the end, he'd had to promise to protect the doctor from his former employer, while he worked on the cure for Lionel.

Over the last few months, through strained conversations Brennan, Marco had discovered that the good doctor had been working in an underground lab that researched powers and how to strengthen them. The goal, as far as Brennan knew, was to make soldiers capable of fighting without the need for traditional weapons.

"Though really, you could use them for anything," Brennan had said. "Assassination, espionage, personal gain."

Marco tried to find out more about the labs Brennan had worked at, and what everyone was doing there, but the man had become tight-lipped when he realized Marco wasn't going to hurt him.

I still need to find out what he knows about those labs experimenting on powered people. What the wrong people could do with someone like me or Lionel...or a dozen like us...

He didn't need to finish the thought, Marco could well imagine the terrible things someone could do with a powered army at their command.

Marco gave the cabbie some of his dwindling cash and waited across from a two-story brick doctors office.

Less than five minutes later, a short, balding man in a

threadbare suit and coat walked down the steps of the building. The doctor stepped into a patch of snow and grimaced, shaking his foot as if water had seeped right through the sole, which it probably had. Marco shook his head and wondered why Brennan didn't spend some of his considerable earnings on decent clothes.

Brennan's small brown eyes darted left and right. He hunched his shoulders against the cold his thin coat let in and made eye contact with Marco, who nodded at him. Dr. Brennan didn't acknowledge him, but instead walked with short, quick steps down the street.

Marco knew the way to Brennan's apartment blindfolded at this point, but still followed at a close distance. The one time he'd lagged too far behind, Brennan had panicked. Better to have the man as calm and focused as possible tonight.

He was a block away when a muffled scream reached his ears, followed by scuffling and the sound of running feet.

"Please, let me go!" said a woman's voice.

Marco glanced at Brennan, who was getting further away by the second, then back at the alley just ahead to his left.

"Damn it," he muttered as another scream rang out.

Marco ran into the alley to see a woman with golden hair surrounded by three tall, broad men.

"Sorry, we have orders, and you know it."

"But...but you could just say that you didn't find me. Please?"

"Nope, boss wants you back, you're one of his favorites."

Marco had heard enough. He let his powers loose, the world changing to a silvery gray color. The shadows wound around the nearest man, barging through the front door of the man's mind. It took one second for Marco to find a terrible memory and make the man relive it. He collapsed to the ground, writhing in pain.

The other men looked down at their fallen comrade in shock just as the shadows wound around both of them. It had been a while since Marco had tried to manipulate more than one mind at once, and the feelings both men harbored for their victim, the malicious delight that came with inflicting pain…Marco gasped with disgust.

For a moment, he wanted to cripple them in a small, subtle way. A just punishment for lives spent hating and hurting. The shadows twirled, as if excited by the thought.

Then Marco grit his teeth, remembering who he was, who he wanted to be. Instead, he dug out their cold, dark memories and plunged both into their own personal versions of hell.

One man screamed and passed out, while the other sobbed like a child and ran out of the alley. The first man was in a fetal position screaming and sobbing when Marco tried to pull the shadows back.

They resisted, crawling toward the blond woman, who was staring in shock at what was happening.

The shadows curled around her ankles, panic flowing from her like a sickly-sweet fragrance. Marco pulled on the shadows, harder this time. They resisted again, but finally let go of the woman and flowed back to him.

When the world turned back to normal, Marco was panting, and sweat was breaking out on his brow, in spite of the piercing cold. One of the men was still laying on the ground, but his cries were quieter now. Marco looked at the woman, who stood frozen to the spot, gaping at him.

"You're alright, I won't hurt you, I swear," he said, reaching out a hand to her. "We should go."

After a moment she put her small hand in his and let him lead her out of the alley.

"Thank you," she said, stepping into the light of the

street lamps. "That was…well, I don't think I've ever seen…thank you."

Marco was speechless for a second.

She was beautiful. Creamy skin flushed from fear and the cold. Her large blue eyes shining up at him, bow-shaped mouth open just a little, golden hair falling around her shoulders and heart-shaped face.

"You're…uh…yeah, you're welcome. You should go home, get someplace safe."

"What's your name?"

"Marco Mayer," he answered before he could stop himself.

"Thank you, Mr. Mayer," she said, then turned and ran off down the street.

He stared after her a moment before panic hit him like a mack truck.

"Shit! Dr. Brennan!"

His long legs made short work of the block he ran down, and soon he was standing in front of Brennan's apartment building.

Marco frowned. Something wiggled around in the back of his mind, making the shadows itch under his skin. He could feel them begin to seep from his fingertips, and drew them back even as he allowed himself to reach out with his senses, just a little.

Something dim and erratic floated around in his mind. Glee, anger…and something else Marco couldn't pinpoint.

As he investigated around Brennan's building, Marco kept his mind open, hoping to find what was brushing against his awareness. The feeling began to intensify as the minutes passed, until his skin burned with the need to use his powers.

Someone was afraid…no…terrified.

Marco grit his teeth as he took the stairs two at a time to Brennan's fourth-floor studio apartment, the muffled sound of hysterical crying just barely discernible. He'd just reached the top landing when an agonizing scream ripped through the air.

Without even trying the door, Marco kicked it open and stopped dead in his tracks.

There was blood splattered all over the apartment floor from knife wounds Brennan was inflicting on himself. Marco stared as Dr. Brennan raised a large butcher knife in both hands and then plunged it into his chest. Another scream tore from the doctor's throat, terror and pain distorting his doughy features.

Marco lunged as Brennan stabbed himself again. His wrist was slippery with blood as Marco tried to wrench the knife free. The smaller man was stronger than Marco expected and before Marco could stop him, the doctor slid the knife across his throat.

A sizable audience was now gathered in the hallway and two women began screaming as Brennan clutched his throat, blood seeping between his fingers.

"Call an ambulance!" Marco shouted, easing the man onto the bloody carpet.

Brennan's pale lips were moving, his small eyes becoming glassy.

"What is it?"

Warm blood seeped through the knees of Marco's pants, but he ignored it and leaned down to try and hear what Dr. Brennan was saying.

"L-Liam…forty-five…sixteen," his voice was wet and thick.

"Who is Liam?"

The doctors eyes closed, but his lips tried to keep moving. "S-Starr…"

"Stay awake, c'mon!" Marco patted Brennan's face, his fingers slick with blood.

"Fl-fl…" Dr. Brennan's lips stopped.

"No, no, no!" Marco shook the blood-drenched man, though he knew it was too late. He gave a shout of anger and sprang up, hands and knees sticky with blood. The after taste of Dr. Brennan's intense fear hung heavy on his mind.

Whoever Liam was, he was the one who had done this to Brennan.

Or rather made Brennan do it to himself, which means a powered person...which probably means his former employer. Damn it!

He grabbed a dish towel and cleaned the blood off his hands as best he could. There was nothing he could do for the man now, and while Marco felt guilty at the thought, he still needed that cure.

Hurrying to Dr. Brennan's desk, he rifled through the papers there, looking for the formula for Lionel's cure, but it was just bills and bank statements.

Damn it! Think, where would it be?

Marco's eyes ran over the room and he bolted to the coffee table.

He jerked open the drawers, but only found cigarettes and old magazines. It took two strides to get to the bathroom, where Marco ripped open the medicine cabinet and drawer, finding toiletries and little else.

This was a studio apartment, so there was no bedroom to search.

But, he does have a Murphy bed.

Marco yanked it down from the wall and shoved his hands under the mattress. But, all he got was a cut from one of the springs. Next, he ran to the kitchen.

As he searched the drawers, he realized how his actions must look to the crowd in the hallway, but he didn't care. He had to find Dr. Brennan's notes.

"And if the damned man had let me be here when he'd

started his work, I'd know where he kept them," Marco said to himself.

Marco slammed the silverware drawer closed, and then his eyes fell on a door to the right of the bathroom, a closet.

"I'm so stupid!"

But before he could take a step towards it, the police came storming in. He had a moment to marvel at how fast they'd arrived before they were pushing him into a nearby chair.

As the police secured the scene and stood over him, Marco stared at Dr. Brennan's body. All the hope he'd felt about getting closer to the cure, the purpose that had driven him through every lonely night, every crappy job — was gone. This was the end.

He buried his face in hands, still red with dried blood.

I've failed.

The police questioned Marco for a good two hours, trying to get him to admit to something. In the end, they had nothing on him, especially since all the witnesses said the same thing: Dr. Brennan had killed himself and Marco had tried to save him.

By the time Marco was free to go it was late and snowing. His mind was numb with defeat as he stepped outside, the falling snowflakes felt like cold feathers on his face. All he wanted was a warm bed and a bottle of scotch, but getting back to his dilapidated apartment would be challenging. He had no money for a cab, and buses wouldn't go to Devil's Own.

Marco sighed, turning to a police officer jogging up the steps. "Do you have a dime? I need to make a phone call."

The police officer gave him some change and rushed into the station.

The payphone on the corner smelled of urine, and the receiver was greasy to the touch, but Marco ignored it. With a cringe he dialed his assistants number and waited as the phone rang four times.

"Hello?"

"Colleen? It's Marco."

"Yeah, I could've guessed. Where are you?"

"Tenth precinct."

She sighed. "What did you do this time?"

"I'm sorry to ask this, but—"

"I'll be right there."

"Thanks."

"Yeah, yeah."

Marco waited just inside the precinct until a clanking car that was more rust than metal pulled up outside. He rushed out and climbed into the passenger side before the car could die. It took three tries to slam the door shut and the car back-fired as they pulled away from the curb, causing three officers to come running out.

"I'm sorry about this," he said.

"What happened?"

Marco pinched the bridge of his nose. "Case gone bad."

Her dark brown eyes slid over to him, full lips quirked in a smile that said she knew he wasn't being completely honest. But, like usual, she didn't press.

Reaching behind her, Colleen threw a plain paper bag into his lap.

"I figured you haven't eaten all day."

His mouth watered at the smell of barbecue chicken and fries.

"You didn't have to do that."

She shrugged broad shoulders. "I got extra, was gonna bring it over tomorrow, anyway."

Marco knew that was a lie, but only nodded.

Colleen was his third assistant, and she'd tolerated him the longest – five months now. He'd done his best to keep her at arm's length, but the tall Negro woman had an uncanny talent for getting him to talk. Before he knew it, Marco was starting to like the idea of having a friend again, even if he couldn't tell her everything.

They rode in silence as Marco scarfed down the food. It was from a small place between Devil's Own and the High Tide neighborhood, one that Marco and Colleen frequented, since they didn't care if one of them was white and the other black.

He was just crumpling up the bag when Colleen turned the corner for his street. Half a dozen people loitered on the frigid sidewalk, some of them in clothes so skimpy Marco wondered how they didn't freeze to death. He felt nervous every time he asked Colleen to be here after dark. He could accept the risk for himself, but he didn't want her getting hurt.

"See you tomorrow," she said, stopping at his building.

Marco darted out, the car once again back-firing as she drove away.

His body ached as he climbed the creaking steps to his apartment on the fourth floor. Someone had broken both ceiling lights above the second floor again and Marco sighed. He'd replaced them five times in the last two months. Though he knew his way by now, it was still frustrating that the people around him couldn't be even moderately decent.

One of the locks stuck as he turned the key, but after jiggling it, the door creaked open. He stared at the peeling black letters on the door: "Mayer Investigations" and made a mental note to repaint them, before closing the door behind him. It was somehow colder in his apartment than outside and he quickly turned the radiator on. It clanked and pinged as if someone were trying to dismantle it, and eventually heat came rushing out.

The only light in the grim apartment was from the small desk lamp he'd left on, but it was enough for Marco to find the bottle of cheap Scotch he kept in his kitchen cupboard. Forgoing a glass, he knocked back a swig and sighed as the liquid burned his insides and warmed his half-frozen limbs.

He began to take off his coat and thought better of it, the apartment hadn't warmed up yet and he was tired of being cold. With a bone deep sigh, he sat in his desk chair and stared at the scratched surface of his desk. The night ran through is mind in a terrible loop. Every smell and sound. The sensation of all those emotions in his mind, a ghostly aftertaste still lingering.

He wrote down the name Dr. Brennan had whispered, along with the numbers and the word 'star'. He'd never come across anyone named Liam in any of his research, and was more than a little unnerved at the thought of someone being able to control another person to this degree.

I might not have come across a 'Liam', but Gerald might have, if Brennan's former employer and Victoria Veran are connected. And that's a big 'if'…

Gerald had been the team doctor when all of them had been in Jet City, trying to do some good. He had healing abilities and was a patient and wise man. In the last year, Marco had come to rely on him, not just for information, but also for solace when he'd hit a dead end or been overcome with loneliness. It wasn't fair, not really. But, he knew it was better than calling Alice.

Marco took another long drink and picked up the phone receiver. Glancing at his watch, Marco cringed, realizing how late it would be Jet City. He was about to hang up when a tired voice answered.

"Gerald?" Marco asked.

There was a pause, a long sigh. "Hello Marco."

"I…I need a favor."

"Are you alright?"

"Yes, well…sort of."

"Do you need me to fly out?"

"No, nothing like that. I need some information," Marco continued. "I've hit a wall here with the list of scientists you gave me and Lionel."

"What kind of wall?"

"The dead kind."

"Oh, I'm sorry Marco – that was all the information I could dig up. I'm not sure what else I can do for you."

"Have you ever come across someone named 'Liam' or 'Star'?"

There was a pause. "No, that doesn't sound familiar, why?"

"Just something a dead man said to me."

"You sure you're alright?"

"Best as can be expected. Are there any other names, any at all that you might be able to find? Last time we talked, you said Alice was doing her own research, is there anything in what she's finding that might point to someone else?"

Gerald paused. "Why don't you call her and ask?"

Marco sighed. "You know I can't."

"I know you won't."

"It's not that simple."

"Yes, well, leaving like you did complicated things."

"I thought you understood."

"I do, but Alice doesn't."

Marco ran a hand over his face, his gut twisting. "I know, and I'm trying to make it right."

"I know you are…" Gerald's voice softened. "But the research she's doing isn't something I can access easily. She's keeping it locked up, even from me. I'll keep an ear open though. If I hear anything, I'll let you know."

"Thank you, Gerald."

"Sure, anything I can do to help."

Marco's hand tightened on the receiver, his mouth becoming dry. There was nothing else to talk about, no other reason to stay on the phone.

Except for one.

"I know you want to ask," Gerald said, his voice sympathetic. "So, go ahead."

"How is she?"

"She's good. Mrs. Frost's illness is hard on her, but she puts on a brave face."

"How long?"

"Soon. There's no way Mrs. Frost will hold on much longer and I can't do anything about it."

Marco cringed to hear the helpless frustration in Gerald's voice.

"I'm sorry," Marco said. "I wish—"

"I know. But you chose to leave... you can't keep doing this to yourself, Marco. You have to accept your life in Metro City or come back here and accept the fallout from what you did. You can't keep straddling two places, two lives. Pick one, and try to be happy."

Marco's body tensed, and he suddenly wanted to be anywhere but on the phone with Gerald.

"I know," he said. "Thanks for the talk, and the help. I know it's late, I should let you go."

Gerald sighed, as if he knew what Marco was really doing.

"Take care of yourself, please?"

"I will," Marco slipped the receiver back into the cradle and lay his head on the desk.

Marco knew Gerald was right. He'd never considered a future without Lionel and Alice though, had never thought he'd have to. Yet here he was, without his best friends, living a life he hated. He only admitted it on nights like this, when hope seemed like a distant dream and the only comfort was a bottle.

There were times when the thought of another day was excruciating, when Marco wished, just for a moment, that everything would fall away and leave him in peace.

CHAPTER THREE

Colleen's thick-soled black boots made hollow echoes on the stairs as she climbed up to her fourth-floor apartment, the smell of roasted meat and cigarette smoke making her nose itch. She wondered why Marco was really at the police station.

She'd known for a long time now that he had a case on the side, that something had been eating at him for longer than she'd known him. There were times Colleen wanted Marco to confide in her, let her be a support or help. Then she'd remember why she'd taken the job in first place: a good cover to investigate her brother's disappearance.

Marco didn't question her, because he had his own secrets. If she made him feel like opening up, maybe he'd start to wonder about Colleen. And that was something she couldn't have, no matter how much she might like the man.

Reaching the door to her apartment, Colleen paused. Her mat was off center, which could only mean one thing.

Cautiously opening the door, she stepped inside.

She always left the light above stove on so she wouldn't walk into a dark apartment, but the lamp by her bookshelf was on as well. The wall to her galley kitchen blocked her view of who might be sitting in the chair next to the lamp, but Colleen could hazard a guess.

Taking her time hanging up her coat so she could steady her heartbeat, Colleen patted her straightened pixie cut, feeling the way it was curling up at the nape of her neck and in little places on the side. She made a quick mental note to see the stylist in Devil's Own and cringed. The woman was dreadful, but the only option. Colleen took a deep breath and walked into the small living room.

She usually found comfort in this room, with its burnt orange walls decorated with paintings and artistic music posters, the worn red and brown area rug, and her mismatched bookshelves. The chair that was currently occupied had been patched so much that Colleen didn't know exactly what the original color was, but the old stuffing and springs molded themselves to her body when she sat in it.

She saw the cigarette smoke just before the person blowing it out. She took a breath to steady herself, a subtle rush of heat shooting through her veins.

The man sitting in the chair was a little older than her, with hair perfectly straightened and greased, the smell of expensive pomade wafting just under the tobacco. His dark skin was smooth in the low light, large brown eyes turning to her in a lazy, unconcerned look.

"Where've you been?" he asked, voice low and gravelly.

"Hello to you too, Rick. Out, what do you care?" she asked, pouring herself a brandy from her meager sideboard.

"I don't." Rick flicked ash into a red tray on the table next to him. "Just curious."

"Did we have an appointment?"

"No, but something has come up."

She stopped mid-drink and looked at him. He met her eyes, a smile tugging on his lips.

"Did you find him?" she asked.

"No, but Tina has a new lead."

Colleen raised a thin eyebrow.

"Tina? You're not calling her Mrs. Knight anymore?"

He took a slip of paper out of his pocket and handed it to her. Colleen read it and sighed.

"Roach? Seriously? Wasn't he one of the first people you talked to about my brother's disappearance?"

"He wasn't a concern at the time, but now we think Andrew saw him just before he disappeared."

Colleen took a drink, and closed her eyes.

The bakery Roach worked at was deep in High Tide, the place she'd grown up in and run from like the devil himself was chasing her. There was only one thing that could drag her back to that neighborhood.

Just the thought of her brother was enough to make Colleen's jaw tense against tears that gathered at her lids and threatened to fall. He'd been missing for almost six months, just before she'd gone to work for Marco Mayer.

Colleen hadn't heard from him or her mother, Tina, since she'd gone to Cambridge, six years ago. Then, the day came when Rick showed up in Desert Springs and told her that Andrew, her brother, was missing and Tina needed her help.

No one else could have gotten her back in Metro City, let alone living in the Devil's Own, right next door to High Tide. But, Andrew was special. He'd been sweet and inno-cent, the one person who had loved her unconditionally in her entire family. He'd also been enamored of the criminal life Grandfather had raised them in, and was prone to getting in over his head trying to prove himself.

"Tomorrow," she said, taking another drink. "I'll see him tomorrow morning."

Rick stubbed out his cigarette and stood.

"You'll need to report to Tina directly on what you find."

She nearly choked on the bourbon. "What? Why?"

"Dunno, it's just what she told me."

"But—"

"Grandfather hasn't gone outside his brownstone all that much in the last year," Rick said, "and Tina's influence has been growing steadily in that time. But if you're really so scared that you'll piss yourself at the thought of running into the old man, Tina still keeps her same appointment at Rachel's Place. Grandfather wouldn't be caught dead there."

Colleen wanted to tell Rick where to go and how to get there, but something else was working in her mind.

If he's bold enough to be talking like this about Grandfather, then Tina must be close to taking power. And, I could actually get my hair done right at Rachel's Place.

She shoved away the sliver of excitement that thought brought up and filed away what Rick said, to examine later.

He frowned at her.

"What?" she asked.

"Nothin'…just…you were always meant to be right beside Tina when the time came. You would make a good right hand."

Colleen took another drink and set the glass down, heat beginning to build in her hands.

"I don't want that life," she said, her voice low. "Never did."

"Not sure I believe that."

"Believe what you want, I'm out."

Rick stepped up behind her. "You sure about that?"

She turned to face him, her eyes narrowing. "What's that supposed to mean?"

He paused. "Tina would never say it, but…she wants you there, where you belong. She needs you there. Once she's able to take over, there's some that won't like it, regardless of who she is and how much she's earned it. Having you beside her…"

Colleen examined Rick, the subtle shift in his tone, what he clearly wasn't saying.

He's nervous…concerned for Tina. Could he…? No…could he love her?

"Tina gave me the out," she finally said.

"Yeah, that's true. But it killed her to do it."

Colleen laughed, a harsh bitter sound. "Tina was relieved to get rid of me. I was her only competition for Grandfather's seat at the table. It was as much for her benefit as mine to send me away."

"Maybe that was true once, but not anymore."

Colleen paused, doubt flowering in her mind.

"Think about it," Rick said, stepping back and walking out the door.

That is the last thing I want to do…but damn! That man got in my head for sure!

Colleen stretched her neck muscles, feeling a headache coming on. She knew that a warm bath and some sleep would help immensely, but there was no way she could relax after Rick's visit.

Instead she poured a little more bourbon and sat in the chair Rick had vacated, the scent of his pomade still lingering on the fabric like an unwelcome reminder that she would never be free of her family.

She chuckled at the word: Family.

Tina had sent Colleen away to England for College, under the pretense of protecting her daughter from a life in the family business. Colleen knew it had more to do with Tina's fear of the powers Colleen had developed. Despite that, she would always be grateful to her mother for that one act.

Getting away from her family had been like being able

to breathe for the first time in her life. How her mother had managed Cambridge was still a mystery, but Colleen hadn't cared at the time. She was free to study art and feel that maybe, just maybe, her life wouldn't be a constant chess game of survival.

Friendship, and love, had been hers. And, like many wonderful things, it had been hers for only a brief time.

Deep into her third year, Grandfather found her.

Though he hadn't discovered her powers, he'd uncovered a secret even more precious. Like a bad dream, the memory surfaced and Colleen cringed.

"You think you're better, girl?" Grandfather had asked all those years ago. *"You are what I made you! You are mine! And anything you do, no matter what, you will always come back to me and what I made you. I ground it into your soul and it's never coming out, you hear me?"*

The empty glass in her hand shattered from the heat that had built up in her. Hot shards landed on her lap and around the chair.

She swore under her breath and cleaned it up, all the while wondering if she ever saw the old man again, would she hold back? Or be what he made her, and unleash hell?

CHAPTER FOUR

Screams came to Marco through the dense gas. The fear and hate flowed into him, constant and forceful. He was drowning in it.

Shadows erupted from his hands and it felt so good. He was tired of holding back, of swallowing the endless waves of emotion and letting it sit in his mind, like a gluttonous black hole.

The shadows rose up, towering and dense. Marco felt clean for a moment, as if he'd vomited all of the putrid feelings into that mass of writhing darkness. And he saw it then, the solution, the way to save Lionel and Alice, and end it all.

So many minds inside rotted houses, and all he had to do was let the shadows bulldoze them.

"It's enough!" Lionel yelled.

"No, it's not!"

Then, as sudden as death, silence.

Marco felt a small hand on his arm and looked down.

That same little boy, only this time his face was painfully clear. Deep set brown eyes stared up at Marco and the child smiled.

"I'll let you win, I promise. And then, we can go get some candy."

"Who are you?" Marco whispered.

The child looked up at him, the face beginning to fade.

"You promised. You promised to keep me safe, to never let them take me."

"I don't understand – who are you?"

The child let go of his arm and drifted away, like someone was pulling him back.

"Find me!"

The shrill ring of a telephone jolted Marco awake. He winced in pain at the stiffness in his neck as he raised his head from the rough surface of the desk. A ghostly taste of emotion clung to his mind, and for a moment, Marco felt certain he knew that little boy. The harder he tried to grab a hold of it, however, the further the knowledge slipped away until only the feeling remained.

The phone continued to ring, piercing the last of the sleepiness as he fumbled for the receiver.

"Hello?" His voice was scratchy, raw.

"You sound terrible," said a concerned woman's voice.

Marco glanced at his watch. It was half past six, his usual time at St. Nic's boxing gym. Allegra, a beautiful Italian woman, who had been his mother's best friend, ran the gym. When Marco had moved to Metro City, the older woman had taken him under her wing. Though he didn't spend too much time with his mother's family, Allegra was different. When Marco was with her, it was almost like having a part of his mother back.

"Hello? You still there?" Allegra asked.

"Yeah…I'm here."

"A little hung over this morning, are we?"

"No," Marco said, his voice a low growl.

The Scotch bottle still had a few swigs left, and though his head ached, it wasn't as bad as some mornings, much to Marco's surprise. If there had been any night tailor-made for getting well and truly drunk, it would've been last night.

"Well, then," Allegra continued, "get over here. Your Aunt Appolonia sent some food for you, and if you don't get it soon, the boys will."

"Fine, fine...I'm on my way."

His mouth was dry, and as he stood from the chair, he felt like someone had twisted his back into knots. An image of Brennan in a bloody heap popped into Marco's mind and a hollow ache settled in his gut.

Giving up had never been an option in all this, but Marco had no idea where to go from here. He was no scientist, and he didn't know anyone who would be able to create a cure out of thin air.

"What the hell do I do now?" he said, running a hand through his hair. Strands fell over his forehead and tickled his eyebrow.

"Alice would say that I need a haircut," he murmured, the ache turning to a pain. "I promised to return Lionel to her...and I keep my promises."

Marco bundled himself in grubby sweats and running shoes, gasping in surprise when he stepped outside. It had snowed quite a bit overnight, a blanket of virgin white concealing the decay around him. For a moment, the beauty of it all took his mind off the mess he'd made of his life, and he smiled.

Then an icy wind hit him and Marco yelped.

"Better get moving before I freeze on the spot."

He jogged the ten blocks to Little Italy, lungs burning with the exertion and cold air, though at least his body was warm.

Turning the corner onto the block where St. Nic's Boxing Gym was located, Marco stopped and took in the cozy neighborhood. He could smell bread from the bakery at the end of the street mixed with coffee from the small café, two doors down. A small magazine stand was untying newly-delivered newspapers, the man swathed in a thick coat and scarf. Soon the quiet streets would be alive with men and women traveling to the markets or to the coffee shop for a game of chess and an espresso.

Brightly colored awnings were frosted with snow, reminding Marco of the massive gingerbread village his mother had made one year. He smiled at the memory, hearing her chiding voice when he'd snapped the gumdrop roof off a house.

A slim man in an apron stepped out of the butcher shop and saw Marco. He raised a hand in greeting and Marco gave him a small nod before jogging toward the building at the end of the block.

A newly painted sign over the green door read "St. Nic's Boxing Gym". The outside was usually papered over with notices for plays, concerts and the like, but Allegra had recently painted it a deep blue and replaced the grimy awning with a bright, white one. The residents of Little Italy may not have wealth to spare, but they took pride in their businesses.

He knew most of these people, or at least they knew him. His mother had grown up here, the jewel of the neighborhood, if his father was to be believed. And when she had died unexpectedly, he and his father had brought her back to be buried. The family had taken to Marco, who had been thirteen at the time. The aunts fussed and fed him cannoli until his insides burst, the uncles had ruffled his hair and smiled in sympathy. One had given him his first taste of wine, which he promptly threw up.

Allegra seemed to have been the only one to notice just how distraught Marco had been to lose his mother. They would talk for hours about how Marco hadn't done anything to cause God to take his mother away. Marco had even begun to believe it and was tempted to tell Allegra about his powers. Some of his memories of that time were fuzzy, like a dream that you can't quite recall. This was especially so when it came to why his father had decided to leave so suddenly.

When Marco returned to Metro City, six months ago, he found out that Allegra had left her job with the orphanage she'd started and taken over her father's boxing gym. Marco had asked only once why she'd left the orphanage.

"Sometimes," Allegra had said, "we are faced with an impossible choice. For me, that choice had…terrible consequences."

The look of regret on Allegra's face had been so painful that Marco had never broached the subject again.

A wave of hot air tinged with the smell of sweat and some kind of cleaner hit Marco the moment he stepped through the door of the gym. His thick sweatshirt, which was so comfortable outside, now felt suffocating. He peeled it off as he walked through the main gym and to the locker room, a few of the regulars nodding to him.

"Hey Marco," said one, a giant of a man who happened to be Marco's cousin. "Missed you at dinner last night."

Marco stopped, guilt gnawing his stomach.

"I'm sorry, Giorgio, I was working."

Giorgio nodded. "Yeah, yeah, we all know how important your work is. Still, I'd like a second chance to beat you at chess."

Marco smiled. "Yeah, well first you have to learn how to play."

"What? I know how to play! Tell him, Dante."

Marco turned to the doorway and saw Dante, the stocky trainer, grinning. His small brown eyes were half hidden under bushy eyebrows that were a strange contrast to his bald head.

"Sorry, Giorgio," Dante said, "moving pieces around a board at random isn't playing chess."

"Yeah, yeah," Giorgio said. "Will we see you next week, Marco? I hear Cicely Morgan is back, and out of mourning. You remember her, right?"

Giorgio made shapely motions with his hands, and then kissed his fingertips.

"Alright, cut that out and get to work on that speed bag," Dante said, his raspy voice sharp. "You know how Allegra feels about that kind of talk."

Giorgio started to walk out, but when Dante's back was turned he smiled at Marco, eyebrows waggling. Marco rolled his eyes and turned to his locker.

Once he had taped his hands and stretched a bit, a light from the nearby office caught his eye. He walked over to the doorway and peered into a room crammed floor-to-ceiling with old banker boxes and filing cabinets. A scratched wooden desk was crammed among the organized chaos, and sitting in a squeaky chair behind it was a woman who could have been his mother's twin.

Wings of gray appeared in her dark hair, which was swept into a simple knot at the back of her head. A faded, but clean and pressed, green skirt suit hugged her mature curves and brought out the olive tones in her square face. Dark brown eyes framed by crow's feet looked up at him when Marco knocked on the always open door.

"Hello there," she smiled, showing a dimple in her right cheek. "You alright this morning?"

Marco ducked his head, shame welling up.

"It's not the first time I've spoken to a hung-over man,"

Allegra said, stepping out from behind her desk, black heels clicking on the cement floor. "But you seem to be doing it much more often these days...and I am worried."

"Allegra—"

"You haven't been yourself all these months and I've given you time, hoping you'd open up to me."

Marco met her eyes. They were so like his mother's that he was taken aback by it sometimes. She patted him on the chest with a well-manicured hand.

"I am not your mother, God rest her..." She crossed herself. "But I promised her that I would always look out for you, be here for you. There's nothing you could ever say that would make me lose respect or affection for you, you know that, right?"

"I do," he said, his mouth dry with secrets.

In that moment, Marco wished he could take off the heavy burden he'd carried all this time and tell Allegra everything. He imagined sitting in her small front parlor, sipping espresso, and telling her everything about Lionel and Alice. About how he'd failed them, and why he could never go back to the life he had before.

Instead, he forced a smile and shook his head.

"You don't need to worry," he said, patting her hand. "I'll find my way. And I'll get those last few boxes out of the storage room too, I just—"

"Don't worry about it. You can keep them here as long as you like. Or, you could just move into the vacant apartment upstairs."

Marco smiled. "And have the aunts dropping by all day? No thanks."

Allegra sighed. "Alright. You better get out there, before Dante has to come looking for you."

Marco nodded and turned away.

"Oh," Allegra said, her worried smile turning a bit

wicked, "your Aunt Stella has left you an invitation to dinner. Apparently, someone special is in town."

"I thought the Aunt's had stopped trying to match-make," Marco said.

"I told them to, doesn't mean they'll listen. If you're not going, you should call her. She was worried last time."

"I will, I promise."

"Would it be so bad?" Allegra asked, the worry back. "You might find someone you could learn to like, if not love."

I already found someone to love. She just doesn't feel the same.

"I better go. Dante hates it when he as to search for me."

Marco turned his back on her and walked into the gym. He found Dante by the speed bags and set up in front of the only empty one.

"You look like shit," Dante said, breaking Allegra's no swearing rule.

"Didn't sleep well," Marco said.

Dante grunted and barked an order at a short young man at the punching bag.

Marco could hear the gasping breaths of the men sparring in the large boxing ring at the center of the gym, the hollow sound of punches against the heavy bags. The quick slap of half a dozen jump-ropes and the thump of speed bags being worked.

Here, the emotions around him were simple, quiet. Marco could feel them, but they were distant, an echo in the back of his mind that gave him a measure of peace he didn't find anywhere else.

Pushing aside all the questions and regrets that the alcohol couldn't wash away, Marco fell into his training like most people do a hot bath. After a while, sweat dripped down his long face and slim chest.

It wasn't until Dante tapped him on the shoulder, that Marco felt jolted back into the world.

"You'll be late for work," Dante said.

"That's what's great about being the boss." Marco took a drink from the canteen Dante handed him. "No one cares if you're late."

"That girl of yours will."

"Colleen? She's used to it by now."

Dante snorted. "You know nothing about women. You should do something about that."

"Not interested in marriage."

"Who said anything about marriage?"

Marco had to chuckle at that.

"Heard Giorgio ask you about dinner last night."

"I was—"

"Working. I know, kid," Dante said, calloused hand clamping onto Marco's shoulder. "I knew your mother, like most people here. She was...special. You're welcome here, wanted even. Just remember that."

"Thank you," Marco said, his voice soft.

Dante nodded, as if knowing this was as good a response as he'd get. "I put your aunt's food in your locker, and don't go out in the cold with all that sweat on ya. At least towel off some."

"Yes, Mom," Marco said, grinning at him.

Dante scowled, though his eyes danced in laughter.

After a brisk toweling off, Marco stepped out into the still frigid morning. The sun was just topping the horizon, pink and purple streaks lancing across a clear sky. The bag of food was heavy in his hand and Marco's mouth watered at the thought of his Aunt Appolonia's fresh bread and preserves.

Shopkeepers and early shoppers were out, braving the cold and a few nodded at him, eyes full of recognition though Marco couldn't remember their names. Jogging across to the magazine stand, he bought a newspaper and glanced at the headline.

SUICIDE AND SCANDAL!
Owner of recently destroyed Lumis Chemical takes his own life after proof of embezzlement and sales of illegal chemicals surface! Possible Russian connection!

Marco looked at the picture someone had snapped of the man's widow being tearfully removed from the home. At first, he just glanced over the picture, then something caught his eye.

Addresses have four numbers...and the street...Isn't there a Starr street somewhere?

The strange sensation he'd felt earlier that morning when trying to remember the boy from his dream returned, making him frown.

Maybe I'm just hungry. Yeah, a little breakfast, then I can think clearly and find out if Brennan was trying to give me an address.

The comforting smell of bread met his nostrils and Marco's stomach cramped. He put up the hood of his sweat shirt and took off at a light jog, hoping the food didn't freeze before he made it home.

CHAPTER FIVE

Colleen sipped the bitter coffee and gazed at the bakery across the street. Anyone else would be freezing in the black-and-red-checked turtleneck dress and long coat she wore. But Colleen wasn't just anyone. The ground around her was free of snow and actually a little warm from the unusual heat her body radiated. The cup of coffee was an hour old, but just as hot as when she'd bought it. If anyone were to look close enough, they'd see small scorch marks on the paper cup where her bare fingers clutched it. It was difficult on the best of days to radiate just the right amount of heat to keep the drink hot, without burning the cup, but when she was nervous, like now, it was nearly impossible.

A man in a threadbare overcoat and pork pie hat walked past her, touching wrinkled fingers to brim. Colleen smiled, but didn't meet his eyes. If even one person recognized her, then Grandfather would know she was back and working with Tina. She didn't want to think about what would happen then.

At last, the man she'd been waiting for stepped out of the side door of the bakery, garbage bag in hand, a scowl on his young brown face.

Colleen put the coffee on a nearby stoop and ran across the street. The young man looked up, a wide grin splitting his round face as he recognized Colleen.

"Well," he said, crossing his arms, "look who came back to the neighborhood. Good to see you, Col."

"It's Miss Knight, Roach."

"Is it? I thought you'd left that behind when you ran with your tail between your legs. And I'm not Roach anymore, you can call me—"

With speed born of years of practice, Colleen punched him square in the face, twisted his arm behind his back and slammed him against the brick wall of the bakery.

"What the hell?" he said.

"Now, that I have your undivided attention. I need information about my brother."

"Andrew? What about him?"

"Have you seen him?"

"Not for about six months," he said, struggling against Colleen's grasp.

"But you saw him six months ago?"

"Yeah. Ow! Shit Col-Miss Knight! Let me go and I'll tell you."

"Damn right you will."

She gave his arm one more twist, and then released him.

Roach scowled at her, rubbing his shoulder. "Andrew came to see me about six months back. Said he was onto something big."

"What exactly?"

"He didn't say."

Colleen took a step toward him and Roach raised his hands. "He didn't! All he said was that he was getting a kind of promotion at work and to keep an eye out for him to hit it big."

"A promotion? Did he say what?"

"No, just that it would be big."

Colleen bit the inside of her lip.

Andrew was a janitor at Lumis Chemical. What kind of promotion could he have been getting?

"Your mother know you're here?" he asked.

"What do you think?" she said, heat building in her body.

He rubbed his jaw. "I think that you should ask her."

"Why?"

"Andrew also said that…shit, can't believe I'm about to tell you this. He said he'd finally be the favorite of the family."

A tremor went through Colleen and she had to consciously rein in her power before she turned into a fireball on the spot.

"Did he say it was Tina or Grandfather that he'd get to notice him?" Colleen asked.

Roach shook his head. "But knowing what I know, I'd guess Grandfather."

Damn it Andrew! That man's acceptance isn't worth shit!

"I swear I don't know anything else," Roach said. "And I'd appreciate it if you left me out of this shit from now on. You'll get me killed."

"Fine, now go get me half a dozen hot rolls and two fresh coffees."

Roach stared at her like she'd gone crazy. All she had to do was raise her fist and take another step toward him to send Roach running into the bakery.

Within minutes he came back out with two white bags. "Here."

"Thanks," Colleen said, knowing she didn't need to tell Roach to keep his mouth shut.

She took the long way back to Devil's Own and tried to shake the adrenaline coursing through her.

The thought that Grandfather had something to do with James' disappearance made her sick, and it wasn't just because of what the old bastard could be doing to James.

I'll have to face him again, I just know it. I barely escaped him last time and now...

Fire raced through her veins and the bag in her started to scorch.

Colleen sat down on a stoop and breathed, picturing her powers flowing backwards in her veins, cooling as they went. It took a few minutes longer than usual to get everything under control. When she had, Colleen realized that this was how Grandfather would beat her. If he could use the fear he'd built into her mind throughout her life, then she wouldn't stand a chance against the old man.

"I'm stronger now...I'm stronger now. I can do this. I can beat him."

She picked up the food, straightened her shoulders and walked on, ignoring the way her stomach still roiled, and the fact that she was sweltering in her coat in spite of the freezing cold air.

Colleen had just managed to bring everything firmly under control by the time she arrived at Marco's apartment bulding. She didn't want him picking up on anything, something he was unnervingly good at.

It wasn't a stretch to say that the fact that Colleen liked Marco, that he treated her as an equal, was a surprise. The few Italians she'd met in her youth had been anything but pleasant to Negroes. But Marco wasn't like most Italians, or most men, for that matter. A fact that made trusting him enough to become true friends a real temptation for Colleen.

The entryway door to the apartment building was blocked by Joe the Drunk, at least that's what she called the man who was always passed out somewhere in the building. Pushing the door gently, Colleen pulled the man all the way inside and ignored the pungent odor coming off him. She laid a hand on his back, warming his clothes just a little, and then tucked a roll inside his coat.

A second-floor apartment door opened as she got to the landing and out came a slight man, his face gaunt and a little sallow, his large brown eyes crinkled around the edges when he smiled at Colleen.

"Hi Henry," Colleen said, handing him a roll. "Hungry?"

He took the roll, fingertips darkened with something that could have been paint or charcoal.

"Thanks, Miss Knight."

"Sure, don't work too hard."

"I won't."

Her long legs took the rest of the stairs two at a time, pert nose wrinkling at the ever-present urine smell on the third floor, and the strange food smells on the fourth.

When she got to Marco's door she wondered what state she'd find her boss in and wasn't at all surprised to see a mostly empty Scotch bottle on his otherwise neat desk. She could hear the sink in the bathroom turning off and hoped that meant Marco had shaved. He looked unkempt with that scruff on his long face.

Colleen's fingertips warmed the remaining rolls and coffee just before Marco walked into the main room, hair still wet, scruff still on his cheeks and chin, clothes neat, though starting to look worn.

"Good morning," she said, handing him a cup of now-steaming coffee.

He took a gulp and winced.

"It's hot," she smirked.

"Thanks," he said. "How are you not freezing in that, don't you own pants?"

She glanced down at her dress and back up, arching one thin eyebrow. "Are you trying to start a fight this morning?"

"Just a question."

Colleen sighed. "Alright, how 'bout we start over? Good morning Mr. Mayer."

"Good morning, Miss Knight."

A slow grin spread on her full lips, brown eyes dancing. "That's better. Now, we have—"

The door opened, without a knock.

Marco and Colleen stared at the woman standing in the doorway.

Golden hair swept into a half up-half down, curvy figure showcased perfectly in gray slacks and a tight black sweater that matched her modest black coat. Her large, light blue eyes stared up at them from under long dark lashes. Full, red lips quirked up in a smile. She looked like a cross between a fashion model and a co-ed.

"You're a hard man to find, Mr. Mayer," she said, her voice teasing.

Colleen was so mesmerized by the beautiful woman she almost overheated her cup of coffee.

"Come in, Miss...?" Colleen said, smiling.

"Delilah Moore," the woman said and stepped into the tiny room.

Colleen took a deep breath to steady herself. She could remember only one other time she'd ever been attracted to another woman so quickly. It was unsettling, especially when her emotions were already prickly from everything else going on in her life.

"I'm afraid I haven't made coffee yet," Colleen said.

"Oh, that's alright, I'm—"

"What are you doing here?" Marco asked, his voice sharp as a knife.

"I need your help, I'm afraid," Delilah said. "More of your help, I should say."

"You know each other?" Colleen asked.

"Mr. Mayer saved my life last night," Delilah said, a dimple appearing in her left cheek as she gave Marco a wide smile.

"And just after that, a man was murdered," Marco said, stepping up to Delilah. "You wouldn't happen to know anything about that, would you?"

Delilah swallowed, the playfulness in her face diminished. "No."

Marco stared at her a moment longer before folding his arms across his chest. "If you're having more trouble with those men, you should go to the police."

"You don't understand, the police can't help me. Only you," Delilah said.

"And why is that?" Colleen asked. Both of them looked at her and Colleen shrugged. "You gotta admit...when someone comes to us instead of the police, something isn't exactly on the up and up."

"You have a point," Marco said, his gaze swinging back to Delilah. "Well?"

Delilah glanced at Colleen.

"My assistant, Miss Knight, is trustworthy," Marco said.

"Alright then," Delilah said, taking a deep breath. "You are...different from most people, aren't you, Mr. Mayer?"

Colleen didn't think Marco could get any tenser, but she was wrong. His hands clenched into tight fists, his long face grew cold and hard.

Have to give this woman credit, she's not even flinching under his stare. But what exactly does she mean by different, is he...? No...could he be?

"Maybe..." Marco finally answered.

The coffee in the cup Colleen still held began to boil.

Marco and Delilah's eyes shot toward her as she raced

for the tiny kitchen, dumping the cup down the sink and taking several deep breaths.

Get a grip!

"Miss Knight?" Marco called. "You alright?"

"Yes, just…yes, I'm fine."

After a few more breaths, she walked back into the living space that doubled as an office.

"Now I see why she's so trustworthy," Delilah said, smiling at Colleen. "You really are clever, Mr. Mayer. A powered assistant for the powered private investigator."

Colleen felt her heart jump to her throat and her entire body went as hot as a day in August. Marco's eyes swung to her, wide and questioning for a moment, and then he relaxed, as if reading Colleen's panic.

Instead of questioning her then and there, however, Marco turned his attention back to Delilah, giving Colleen a chance to regain control.

God bless him for leaving me be for a minute!

"You've been following me? Why?" Marco asked.

Delilah put up her hands and gave Marco a nervous smile.

"To make sure I could trust you, that you were what my associate thought you were. Namely, someone like me. A person with powers. I had to be sure, Mr. Mayer. And when you hear my story, you'll understand why."

"And why should I give you the time of day? If you've been following me, you could've had something to do with Dr. Brennan's death last night."

Colleen saw a flash of recognition in Delilah's eyes, and then it was gone.

"I didn't though," Delilah said, "I swear it. I need your help and I think I can make it worth your while."

Marco gave a heavy sigh and leaned against his desk, brows drawn in thought.

"Alright, spill," he finally said.

Delilah smiled. "I can give you something that you need. Something that you lost last night."

"And what would that be?" he asked.

"I have a…friend…who was a chemist with Lumis Chemical—"

"What?" Colleen blurted. Delilah stared at her, mouth open. Colleen paused, feeling Marco's questioning gaze on her. She never spoke up in client meetings, unless it was to ask questions about payments or something other such benign thing.

"Colleen?" Marco leaned toward her as she shook her head.

"I…my brother worked there."

"Did he get caught in the fire?" Marco asked.

Colleen shook her head. "No, he…he went missing six months ago."

"Let me guess," Delilah said. "He went to work one day and never came back?"

Maybe she's more lethal than pretty.

"That's a very specific question," Colleen said, taking a step toward the woman.

"Forgive me, I just have…let's say, unusual knowledge about that place. Was your brother powered as well?"

Colleen felt Marco go absolutely still next to her, and her own breath hitched at the question. She'd always wondered if Andrew had powers, but he'd never said anything, nor had Tina.

If he does and Grandfather found out…

"Who are you?" Colleen said, unable to keep the fear from her voice.

"You don't need to be afraid or suspicious of me," Delilah said.

"And why is that?" Marco asked.

"Because once you hear me out, you'll realize I'm your last chance to help your friend."

Any attraction Marco might have felt for the gorgeous woman in front of him disappeared with those words. He didn't understand how she knew anything about him or Lionel or the cure, but the very fact that she did made her valuable. And dangerous.

"What do you know about it?" he asked quietly, folding his arms across his taut belly.

"I know that Dr. Brennan was very close to finishing the cure for your friend's — condition. And that someone killed him last night."

Marco felt Colleen's intense gaze on him. He'd grown fond of the woman over the last few months and was surprised at how hurt he felt that Colleen hadn't trusted him with her secret.

I haven't exactly been forthright with her either. Though after she finds out what I can do, it might not matter. She might just take off.

"I'm getting annoyed, so cut to the chase," Marco said.

"Alright," Delilah said. "Where should I begin?"

"How do you know Dr. Brennan?" Marco asked.

"He worked for the same group my friend and I did. I knew him through that work."

Marco's heartbeat quickened. Maybe now he'd find some answers about who Brennan had been working for and be able to stop them.

"What work was that?" he asked, keeping his voice neutral.

Delilah paused. "There is a group that takes powered orphans, experiments on them, brainwashes them, and turns them into weapons. Dr. Brennan and the man I escaped with, Dr. Trace, were two of the men tasked with... enhancing...our abilities."

Marco's eyes widened and he took a deep breath. He hadn't expected this detail, not in the least.

"Our?" Colleen asked.

"Yes, I was taken when I was nine. I lived most of my life in the labs, doing…well, whatever they ordered me to. And I need…I want a new life."

It was the first time since she walked in the door that Marco felt like he'd seen something real, and not rehearsed, from Delilah.

"If this Dr. Trace did that to you, why would you want to go anywhere with him?" Colleen asked.

"Because he helped me escape the night of the fire at Lumis Chemical."

"Where is he now?"

"Unfortunately, Dr. Trace is too frightened to leave the temporary lodgings we found. He insisted on waiting until I'd secured your help."

"Dr. Brennan never told me who the people in charge of this were," Marco said.

"And I'm afraid I can't either," Delilah answered. "The highest-ranking person I knew was the one who ran the lab I lived in, and who was in charge of the tasks I was sent on. He wouldn't have had much in the way of power."

"Who was the 'boss' those men mentioned last night?"

Delilah flushed, blue eyes sparking. "Someone whose name I never knew and I only saw twice. He might be higher in the leadership, but…I have no idea what his name is or anything about him."

"What did he look like?"

"Is this really necessary?" she said, her voice sharp. "I need your help and you cross examine me as if I'm a criminal."

Marco felt shame lance through him and sighed.

"I'm sorry, and you're right. But, what you're describing, what little I got from Dr. Brennan about this, it's disturbing to say the least. What someone could do with a group of powered people—"

Delilah laughed, a dry, bitter sound. "A group implies a small number. I was one of almost fifty in one facility."

Marco stared at her, the words hitting him like cold water. "You...you're telling me that..."

"Dear god," Colleen whispered.

"Look," Delilah said. "I will tell you everything I know about the facility, about the people that are doing this. I'll even describe the bastard that I met those two times, in addition to providing you with what you need for your friend. But, not unless you help me."

It was never Marco's way to use his powers on just anyone, and especially not for selfish reasons like this. But he had to know if Delilah was telling him the truth. He refused to be dragged into something that would keep him from helping Lionel.

So, he reached out, just a little, his shadows shifting under his skin, not revealed to anyone. He felt the barest hint of fear, fatigue and something else...something—

Her eyes met his and she held his gaze.

Lust...

It brought a flush to his skin and he turned away.

Go poking around in someone's mind and that's what you get Marco.

"Alright," he said, taking a sip of his now cooled coffee, "why did you come to me?"

Delilah took a deep breath, her shoulders relaxing. "Because you are the only one I know like me, with powers. I can't trust anyone else not to turn us over to the police, or think we're crazy. We need to get out of the city and we can't do it alone. When we are safe, Dr. Trace will send you what you need."

"No. He'll give it to me before you leave Metro City. I've

come too close too many times to let you just leave and trust that it'll all work out."

"Very well, I believe we can work something out."

"Do you have money?"

Delilah nodded. "Dr. Trace has enough for us to start a new life, he has it with him. We will need a safe place to stay before our train tomorrow night, the place where he is now won't stay secret for long."

"I just have the one bedroom, but you can stay here."

"Thank you."

"I need to know," Colleen said, her voice rough. "What does Lumis Chemical have to do with this? And where is my brother?"

"Lumis is a front," Delilah said. "On the main floors it's all business, a respectable chemical research facility, or at least it was. But they also have underground labs, where they keep the children and their research team."

"Is the underground lab still in use?" Marco asked.

"It's possible. The fire was mainly above floor, but it caused plenty of panic in the labs."

"You said children," Colleen continued. "But my brother is nineteen."

Delilah's gaze became sympathetic. "Then, I'm sorry. He must've had a very special ability, one they thought they could exploit, but the serum used to strengthen abilities tends to kill adult patients."

Marco saw Colleen take the words like a bullet to the chest. She turned away, hand to her mouth.

"I'm sorry," he said, putting a hand on her shoulder and immediately removing it. Her body was hot to the touch, not just warm but almost…

"Don't touch me," she said, moving away.

Marco stared at her, beginning to realize why the food she brought was always piping hot in the middle of winter.

Why she was perfectly alright in skirts and dresses, without the thick tights every other woman wore.

Not here, not now. I can talk to her later.

"Alright," Marco said, turning back to Delilah, "Miss Moore, you stay here while I get Dr. Trace."

"He won't see you without me, I'm sorry."

Marco sighed. "Fine, then you'll come with me. Colleen—"

"I need to go see...someone," she said, turning back around.

Marco swore he saw something like orange light in her brown eyes, but it was gone too quick for him to be sure. He wanted to argue with her, but Colleen had never so much as taken a sick day in all the time she'd been with him. Considering she just found out her brother was likely dead, Marco didn't have the heart to make her stay.

Colleen threw her coat on and beat him to the door.

"I'll be right back," Marco said to Delilah, bolting after Colleen.

Colleen ran down the stairs and burst out of the front door. Marco could feel heat coming from her as he ran behind her.

"Colleen," he said.

"I have to go."

"I know," he said, trying to grab her arm.

She moved away, refusing to look in his eyes.

He opened his mouth to say something and saw steam rising from the iced over sidewalk where Colleen stood.

She must've seen it too because she started to walk.

"I'll be back in a few hours," she said over her shoulder.

Marco could see her footprints in the ice, a strange melted path through the ice and snow.

The phone was ringing when Marco stepped back into his office.

"Hello?" he said.

"You got my pictures?" a gruff voice asked.

Marco sighed. "Yes, Mr. Banks, I can deliver them to you today if—"

"I don't get home until tonight and I don't want my wife knowing I hired you. She might decide to cover her tracks. Tomorrow. Eleven. Don't be late!"

Before Marco could respond, Mr. Banks had hung up.

"I hope you don't mind," Delilah said from the kitchen. "But I started some coffee."

The bubbling sound of the stove top percolator reached Marco's ears seconds before the heavenly smell of coffee.

"Not at all," Marco said, shoving his hands in his pockets.

"I couldn't help but notice that for a bachelor, you have a surprising array of spices."

"I like to cook."

Delilah arched an eyebrow. "Really? And no one has snatched you up yet?"

Marco felt color rise to his cheeks. "Women tend to like a man with a steady income."

"I would've thought in your line of work you'd come in contact with plenty of wealthy women."

"Perhaps."

Delilah smiled at him and nodded. "I see. A gentleman. Curiouser and curiouser."

"We aren't that rare."

"Mr. Mayer, in my experience, true gentlemen are as rare as can be."

"And what experience would that be?" he asked before he could stop himself.

Delilah's eyes shuttered and she turned away. "Coffee's almost ready. Do you take cream?"

Marco inwardly cursed himself for prying and shook his head. "Just sugar. Shouldn't we be getting to Dr. Trace?"

"Not yet. I told him late morning, if we show up early, he won't trust it. We have time for a coffee."

Marco accepted the steaming cup she offered him and tried to force away his growing discomfort. He was used to a certain level of emotional distance from his clients, oftentimes bordering on disgust. And he certainly wasn't used to mistrusting them and feeling attraction all at once.

"Problem, Mr. Mayer?" she asked, full lips curling into a playful grin.

"Hmmm?"

"You haven't taken a sip and you're staring at me like I'm something to be studied."

Nicely done, Marco! Snap out of it!

"Sorry," he said, setting the cup down on his desk, "I'm just tired. If we have time, I do have some work to do, so…" He gestured to the lopsided couch. "Make yourself comfortable."

"Thank you."

Marco settled behind his desk, trying his best to focus on the papers in front of him instead of the leggy blond sipping coffee and reading one of his paperbacks.

After a few minutes, he could already tell it would be a losing battle.

CHAPTER SIX

Tears threatened to blind Colleen as she walked with long, quick strides down the street – to where, she wasn't sure. She just needed to get out of the apartment in case she lost control. It had happened a few times when her emotions got the better of her. And the last thing she wanted was to hurt Marco.

The relatively empty sidewalks soon gave way to places more populated, though just barely. People passed her, eyes down or far away, ignoring her existence, and she liked it that way.

Thoughts of her brother shot through her mind like so many bullets, painful and sharp. No matter how she tried to stop them, they came anyway. She allowed herself to get so lost in memories of her younger brother's laugh and his quiet sweet nature that she didn't see the police car until it pulled up next to her, spraying snow onto her legs.

She jumped from the sudden cold and stopped.

"Where you going, sweetheart?" asked a round-faced officer.

Colleen swallowed. "Beauty parlor."

"Beauty parlor? You seem to be in quite a hurry for just a new haircut."

"It's cold."

The officer got out of the car, his small eyes running up and down her body.

"It is, isn't it? Why don't you get inside, I'll give you a lift?"

Fear and anger shot through her, bringing the heat of her powers with it.

She shook her head. "Thank you, but I'm alright."

The officer stepped closer, his hand running down her arm. "Get in the car. Don't make me ask again."

Colleen could feel the fire inside of her building and tried to calm down. It wasn't the first time she had to get away from a man who thought he could do whatever he wanted to her. But, it was the first time it was happening after finding out her brother was likely dead.

"I-I…"

The officer's thick fingers dug into her arm, and then he immediately let her go.

"What the hell?" he said, a shocked look on his face.

"I need to go," she said, turning away, heart pounding in her ears.

She could feel the heat burning in her veins like a rising tide of fire. The last time it had been this strong it hadn't ended well for anyone involved.

"No, you don't!"

The officer pulled on her coat, sending Colleen off balance and sprawling into the snow-covered side walk, her knee banging hard onto the cement.

He bent down and pulled up on her coat collar.

"Get in the car, you damn freak!"

The world looked as if it were on fire in Colleen's vision, and heat rushed into her hands.

"Go away, please!" she said.

But he didn't. Instead he yanked her to her feet and spun her around.

Colleen kept her hands clenched, willing her power to come back under control. In a moment, she'd lose the battle, and flames would leap from her finger tips.

Please, please, please…get control!

The officer opened the car door and his radio crackled, a voice letting loose a stream of words that Colleen didn't follow.

"Leave her," said another officer in the passenger seat. "We need to go, officer needs assistance."

The officer looked about to argue when more words came over the radio.

"You get a pass," he said, sneering at her. "But if I see you again, you and I are going to finish what we started."

He shoved her and Colleen almost slipped again. The car sped away, spraying more snow onto her wet legs and dress.

People gave her a wide berth as they walked, not looking at her or acknowledging anything that had just happened. Colleen's body trembled, though not from the cold. Steam began to rise off her, the unspent heat seeping out and drying her legs and dress. It was a welcome distraction from the throbbing in her knee.

All she could do, was stand there for several minutes, trying to get past the confusion and anger of the assault. When she managed to get walking again, she stumbled and ended up leaning against a nearby building, the brick old and grungy. She took gulping breaths to calm herself and did her visualization exercise to get her powers under control once more. After a few minutes, her legs stopped shaking and she felt like she could walk without falling down.

"Are you all right?" said a voice behind her.

Colleen spun around to see a beautiful woman around her mother's age, her dark brown face tense with concern.

"I...I'm fine."

The woman pressed her lips together and sighed. "You sure? I have a shop not too far from here, you could sit for a little bit, collect yourself."

"No, thank you. I need to be going."

"Okay then."

Colleen looked past the woman to the street beyond, making sure the police car wasn't waiting somewhere nearby after all. The woman must've seen the fear in Colleen's face, because she put a large calloused hand on Colleen's arm and squeezed.

"He's not here anymore," she said, a grim smile appearing on her face. "And I wouldn't worry about him anyway. Men like that, they tend to get what's coming to them."

Colleen laughed, devoid of any mirth and shook her head. "What world do you live in?"

The woman's smile widened. "I know what you mean. But trust me, he'll get his. You take care."

"I will," Colleen said, watching the woman walk away.

After another minute or so, Colleen decided to walk back out onto the sidewalk. It was still early for Tina's standing appointment at the beauty parlor, and Colleen didn't want to show up there looking such a mess.

I'll go home and change, then take care of this. Maybe... Maybe Tina knows something else and Andrew isn't dead.

Colleen was surprised to discover that she actually cared what the women at Rachel's Place thought about her after all these years. She changed clothes three times before settling on an orange and red skirt, with a black turtleneck and boots.

As she crossed the invisible border from Devil's Own into High Tide, Colleen felt her senses heighten, every sound and smell assessed for the possibility of threat. It was an old habit, one that had served her well many times.

After a block of doing this and nothing happening, Colleen started to relax. Though she'd been in High Tide earlier that morning, she hadn't let herself really take it in. She noticed the pride people took in the old neighborhood. It showed in how they took care of their streets and old buildings, in the sidewalks that had been shoveled. She saw a young man helping a woman with two small kids down a slippery stoop. Yes, some had garbage in the gutters and bums sleeping in their alleys, but every neighborhood had its ugly spots. High Tide had fewer than Devil's Own.

Colleen looked up at the empty window boxes that would be filled with red and pink flowers in the summer, sometimes kitchen herbs, too. Thin, but well-pressed curtains would flutter in the hot breeze and children would chase the rickety ice cream truck, hoping it would stop.

There were good memories here, she realized with some shock.

After a meandering walk down the block, she came to a cheerful yellow sign with curling white and blue script: Rachel's Place, and just under it, the sign obviously repainted many times with pride: Authorized Agent Mme CJ Walker's System & Preparations. She stood across the street from it, staring past the clear windows and into the yellow and blue interior.

I wonder if Rachel is still running the place. She must be... sixty, now? Good god, that can't be right!

The door opened and out stepped a grinning woman, patting her newly straightened and styled hair. It was perfect, just like every style created in the salon.

Colleen took a deep breath and crossed the street. She paused with her hand on the door knob, then turned it. The bell over the door chimed and half a dozen pairs of brown eyes turned to her. They all stared and Colleen felt heat rise to her cheeks.

"Well, I'll be," said a gray-haired woman with a straightening comb in her hand. "Colleen Knight?"

Colleen smiled, forcing her heartbeat to slow down. "Yes, Mrs. Strong, it's me."

After that, the quiet that had descended on the place when she'd entered shattered, as six women tried to hug her at once.

"Give the child room to breathe!" said a voice from a doorway at the back of the shop.

Colleen knew that gravelly commanding voice anywhere.

The women stepped aside and made room for a tall, white-haired woman with a wide grin on her dark wrinkled visage.

Rachel Pole had been running the salon since before Colleen was born. She used the very last of the meager money her husband left her when he died and opened the shop. Everyone said she was crazy. But in a year, her shop was one of the most successful business on the block. Sometimes women waited hours just for a touch up.

"Hello, Mrs. Pole," Colleen said, tears itching her eyes.

"Oh, you come here now!" she said, enveloping Colleen in a strong hug. "I never thought I'd see you again."

The smell of pomade, relaxer and Rachel's homemade apple pie surrounded Colleen, making her feel like a child on a Saturday afternoon all over again.

"Oh, now," Rachel said, stepping away and wiping her eyes. "I can't believe you are here! What do you need? Let me see."

Before Colleen could protest, Rachel had spun her

around and was looking her pixie cut over. Rachel gave a few grunts and a click of her tongue.

"Who have you let do this to you? Your kitchen is turning back and so is this here, and you need a good shampoo. Come on now, you sit in my chair, let me take care of you."

"Mrs. Pole, I actually…"

"What? You don't have time to take care of yourself?"

"No, that's not it, I was just wondering if my mother is here?"

"Hmmm…Debbie, what time is Mrs. Knight's appointment?"

"Right about now, I'd say," said Debbie as she looked out the window.

A shining black car had pulled up and a woman stepped out. She was average height; her curvy body clad in a dark blue and brown skirt, and a brown coat trimmed in fur. A hat was perched on her head, hiding her hair. She opened the door to the shop with a smile that showed a small gap in her two top front teeth.

Colleen felt like a child once again when her mother's shrewd gaze found her, and this time it wasn't a pleasant feeling.

The chattering in the shop once again ground to halt, all eyes on the two women. Everyone knew what Tina Knight did for a living, though in this place, none of that mattered. It was an unspoken rule that there was no rich or poor, no good or bad people in Rachel's place. Her philosophy was that all who stepped through the door to her shop were equal and deserved to feel like a queen, if only for a few hours.

"Well," Tina said, the alto timbre of her voice as smooth and beautiful as Colleen remembered, "Colleen, I'm glad you got my message. It's been too long since I've seen you."

Tina leaned in to give Colleen a peck on the cheek, the action full of unspoken things.

"Yes ma'am, it has been."

"You look well," Tina said, hanging up her coat.

Colleen let Rachel take her to a chair in front of one of the shampoo bowls. The room was still too quiet, as if she and her mother were the actors in some play that everyone had been dying to see.

"Thank you, I am."

Tina sat down in Debbie's chair. "That job agrees with you?"

"Yes."

"What job is that?" Debbie asked, her voice a little too cheerful.

"I told you about that didn't I?" Tina asked, a sharp undertone in her voice. "She's a secretary for a private investigator over in Devil's Own."

A couple of the women gasped.

"Devil's Own?" Rachel asked as she began to massage Colleen's scalp.

"It's not so bad," Colleen said.

"What's your boss like?" asked one of the women, wincing as the hot comb was pulled through her hair.

"He's nice and hard working."

"He's Italian," Tina filled in.

More gasps.

"What are you working for an Italian for?" someone else asked.

"If he hired her he must not be so bad," someone else said.

"He's very nice," Colleen said. "He's not like some of the ones I know you're talking about."

"Must not've been raised around here," Debbie said.

"He has family here, but..." Colleen paused, realizing that she had no idea if Marco was from here or not.

"Maybe Tina would like to talk to her daughter without a bunch of interruptions," Rachel said.

"Oh, it's all right, Mrs. Pole," Tina said. "I was going to treat her to a cup of coffee and cherry pie at the diner after we're done here. You all catch up with her."

Colleen swallowed. A morning of mother-daughter bonding hadn't been part of the deal.

What is going on? Is her real purpose to let Grandfather find me? No, that doesn't make sense. I hope.

"I've heard most private investigators are crooks," said someone, snapping Colleen out of her thoughts. "Or worse...perverts."

"Come on now," Debbie said. "You really think our Colleen would work for...um...someone like..."

"Debbie, it's alright," Tina said, her voice thick with amusement. "We all know that Colleen doesn't work for crooks."

Nervous laughter filtered throughout the shop and Colleen felt her palms become warm.

"Now, nothing wrong with honest work," Rachel said as she rinsed Colleen's hair. "No matter if it's here or...Devil's Own. And I'm sure, whatever she's doing, it's honest. That's our Colleen, as Tina said. Now, let's not forget what we were talking about before Colleen walked through that door."

"I already said I was gonna register to vote! I just don't have a ride down to the place," Debbie said.

"That is not true," said one of the stylists. "I offered to take you."

"You drive like a crazy woman, I'm not getting in a car with you!"

Everyone chuckled and started chatting about their children and how some of them were starting to wear their hair "natural."

"Nothin' natural about it!" said a woman to Colleen's right. "They look unkept, it's disgraceful!"

As Rachel's swift fingers began to work the rich-smelling pomade into Colleen's hair, she met Tina's eyes in the chair next to her.

A memory flashed in her mind.

Saturday morning, sunny but cold. She held Tina's hand as they walked to Rachel's Place. It would be the first of many such trips. Colleen had felt grown, important.

Though I admit, I missed feeling my mother's hands in my hair, hearing her hum along to the radio, the smell of that morning's breakfast in the air, and her perfume.

"Been a while hasn't it?" Tina said, her voice pitched low.

"Yes," Colleen said, the barest smile on her lips.

By the time Rachel was done with Colleen, she felt more relaxed than she could remember being in years. Her hair was sleek and shining, the heady scent of the shop floating around her.

"Thank you, Rachel," Tina said, handing over some money to the woman. "This will cover Colleen as well."

"I can—" Colleen began.

"Nonsense, my treat."

Colleen paused. In her world, there was no such thing as a gift without strings.

"Thank you," Colleen said.

Tina nodded and slipped into her coat.

"Now, let's get that coffee."

Rachel grabbed Colleen in a tight hug that brought unexpected tears to Colleen's eyes.

"Don't be a stranger, you hear?" Rachel said.

"I won't," Colleen said.

The other women in the shop said their good-byes from either behind the chairs or sitting in them as Colleen and Tina walked out the door.

"Come on," Tina said. "I need to talk to you."

"I need to talk to you, too."

Tina eyed her with a hint of suspicion and nodded. They walked the half block to the diner and sat in a faded, red leather booth with a clean but old linoleum table. Tina ordered them coffee and cherry pie. Colleen was bracing herself for awkward small talk when their order came to the table in a matter of moments.

They sipped their coffee and, though Colleen had always loved the cherry pie at this diner, she could only pick at it.

How do I tell her Andrew is likely dead?

"You're probably wondering why I've asked you to come here," Tina said.

Colleen nodded, grateful that her mother was going first.

Tina met her daughter's eyes with a look of intensity that made Colleen want to look away. Years of experience told her not to, so she held the stare with one of her own.

"You've changed," Tina said.

"Of course, I have. Is that why you've given me a trip down memory lane?"

"No, it's just an observation, a compliment even, if you'd stop being so rude for five minutes. I swear I taught you better."

Colleen could feel her shoulders start to climb to her ears and forced them to stay straight. She had cowered enough to this woman when she was younger, she would not do it now.

"You did," Colleen admitted. "You also taught me other things, and I don't feel like being played with, so tell me why I'm here."

"Something has changed since last night and I want you to stop looking for Andrew. Walk away, leave it alone."

Of all the things Colleen had expected, this was the last thing.

She frowned at Tina. "Why?"

"Because I asked you to."

"No, I'm not a child anymore, you don't get to use that reason."

Tina squared her shoulders and looked down her nose at Colleen. Her expression made Colleen's heart pound in her chest.

"You will do as I say," Tina said, her alto voice soft with menace.

Colleen forced herself to keep eye contact with Tina. "Tell me why."

Tina sighed, a sound filled with frustration. "There are other factors. Ones I do not want you involved with."

"Is...Is he...?"

"Dead?"

Colleen nodded, wondering if her mother knew already. "No."

"You know that for certain?"

"Of course I do, what kind of question is that?"

Then Miss Moore was wrong, he's alive.

Her relief was painfully short lived.

If Tina is asking me to walk away, that means Andrew is in even more trouble than I thought. And Tina knows what it is. I hope to god it's not what Delilah described. Andrew being used like a lab rat.

"Does it have anything to do with Andrews' powers and Lumis Chemical?" Colleen asked.

Tina took a bite of pie, her lips scraping along the tines of the fork as if she were savoring it. Her expression didn't change, her body remained as relaxed and strong as before. The signs that something was wrong, that Collen had gotten too close to a secret were almost impossible for anyone to see. Anyone, that is, except Colleen, who had spent a lifetime studying Tina's every move.

Colleen leaned forward, fear for her brother overriding any trepidation she might have felt at challenging Tina.

"What do you know?" she asked.

"That if you go poking around, you'll end up in a cage, like an animal. You want that?"

"Is that what's happened to Andrew?"

"Damn it, girl," Tina said, brown eyes bright with anger. "You need to walk away from this."

"You brought me into it!"

"And now, I'm taking you out of it."

Colleen sat back, mouth hanging open as she realized what Tina was trying to do.

"You're...You're protecting me?"

"You don't have to sound so surprised. It's not the first time."

"But...why?"

Tina set her fork down with a sigh. "I know you think I'm a monster—"

"I never said..."

"You never had to. I may not have protected you from everything you wanted me to, because I was trying to make you strong, so you could survive. But there are somethings I can and will protect you from. And what Andrew got himself involved in, is one of them."

"If that's true we can't just leave him like that."

"I'm not. You're just going to have to trust me on this."

"Let me help. My boss, he might be able to—"

"No," Tina said, her voice sharp with finality. "You are done with this."

Colleen knew she'd gotten as far as she was going to with Tina. Anything else would just make her angry, and that was something Colleen would rather avoid.

But if Andrew is connected to what Lumis has done to Miss Moore, maybe I can get some answers from her before she leaves town. And if the underground lab is still in operation…

"I have to go," Colleen said, taking money out of her purse.

"My treat," Tina said. "Remember?"

Colleen hesitated, and then nodded. "Thank you."

"My pleasure. Be careful, Colleen."

She heard what Tina was really saying under the cordial concern: Stay away from this.

Colleen forced a smile. "Of course, you as well."

Tina nodded and dabbed her lips with the paper napkin.

Colleen's mind spun as she walked out of the diner. If she could somehow get her brother or prove what was happening, and let the police sort it, then she'd be able to save Andrew before Grandfather found out he was powered.

Then we can leave and go somewhere else. Maybe London or back to Desert City. We can have a normal life. Well… maybe not normal. But a life.

She was so preoccupied she didn't notice the man stepping out from the shadows.

CHAPTER SEVEN

Weak sunlight broke through the clouds as Marco and Delilah traversed the slick sidewalks later that morning. He hazarded a sideways glance at her, a little disconcerted that he could detect so little emotion from her. Even when he didn't use his powers, his sense of other people's emotions would slip through. Usually, they were benign, sometimes not. Right now, he'd expected excitement, or at the very least, fear. But all he felt was a low quiver-like sensation from her, as if Delilah's emotions were boxed up somewhere inside, tightly held.

The one thing he did feel, however, was awkward walking next to a beautiful woman in complete silence.

"So," he said, trying his best to sound professional, "how did you escape whoever was holding you?"

She hesitated, stepping out of the way of a staggering man, who reeked of urine and beer.

"Some of us are allowed to go out into the world for brief periods, in order to do our missions," she said, her voice hard beyond her years. "I looked for opportunities, people that might be able to aid me both inside the labs and out in the city. Someone approached me about causing a large enough distraction that I could escape, and I took the opportunity."

"You mentioned that there was more than one lab, were you always in the same place?"

"For the most part, though I've occasionally been allowed to spend a night or two in an apartment as part of a mission. I've heard of the other labs. There's three of them in three separate cities. The Metro City one is the largest."

"I'm surprised you're not more frightened of being out on your own."

"You mean since I was controlled and tortured in an underground lab for most of my life?"

Marco swallowed. "I'm sorry that must've sounded insensitive."

"Yes, but understandably curious. And no, I'm not afraid. I was allowed out more than others."

"Though not with the freedom to do what you wanted. To see life going on around you and not be able to participate...that must've been brutal."

"Yes, it was," she whispered.

"I'm sorry that happened to you."

Her lips curved up into a wry grin. "Pity, Mr. Mayer?"

"No. You're obviously strong, despite what happened to you. It's compassion."

"And fear. You don't want these people to do anymore damage to powered people."

"Of course not."

"Then, you are far braver than I."

"How so?"

She stopped and looked up at him.

"Because there's nothing, absolutely nothing, on this earth that would compel me to face these people again. You want to challenge them, take away their favorite toys, as it were. If you were an ordinary man, they'd simply kill you. But you're not. And if they catch you...if they catch you...

they'll dismantle you until your own mother wouldn't recognize you."

Marco's mouth went dry and his heart raced, as her words sunk in. He'd faced demons before, in Jet City. The last one had cost him everything and he'd lived the last year believing that if he could survive that, he could survive anything. What Delilah described, however, was something Marco had never imagined.

"Just think before you act," she said, walking again. "No one expects you to be a hero."

No...no, they don't.

"Where is the apartment where the good doctor is staying?" he asked after a few minutes.

"16th and Roosevelt."

It was further than Marco would have liked in this weather, but not far enough to warrant a cab. He shoved his hands in his pockets and walked on.

They didn't speak again until they were almost there. Delilah was keeping pace with Marco when she slipped on some ice. He reached out and grabbed her, bringing her body against his in the process.

He could smell her perfume, subtle and flowery, like the first blossoms of spring. She looked up at him through thick lashes and grinned.

"Thank you, Mr. Mayer, I think you can let me go now."

His hands released her and he stepped back.

"Yes, sorry, I...are you...?"

"I'm fine, thank you. The apartment is just up this way."

They crossed one street and waited for the light to turn. Just before it did, Marco felt a stab of terror pierce his mind. He gasped, taking control of the feeling, dampening its impact on his senses.

He turned to Delilah, shocked at how strong and sudden her emotions were.

"Oh god," she said, her face crumpling as if she were about to cry.

"What?"

Delilah turned away and darted into the shelter of a florist's shop. Marco followed her inside, the scent of flowers thick in the air.

"There are three men in dark suits. One leaning against a green car, the other two are around the corner from the apartment building on the corner, where Dr. Trace is. They're from the lab."

Marco looked around, trying to be nonchalant and saw the men she meant. All three were burly and dressed exactly the same. One of them was taller than the other two by six inches, at least, and looked broad enough to lift a building.

"Do you know any of them?"

Delilah looked over Marco's shoulder and swore.

"The tall one, he's powered. They call him the Six Man."

Marco almost laughed. "What?"

"He can duplicate himself into five copies, who are invincible unless you take out the original."

It suddenly wasn't so funny.

"You think Trace is still in there?"

"I don't know," she admitted. "They might be waiting for me. Damn, I thought I had more time!"

"What do you mean?"

"Since the fire they've been trying to track down those of us who escaped, but I didn't think I was high profile enough to warrant one of their special teams."

"Is there a back way into the building?"

She bit her lip as she considered the question.

"I don't think so but there's a fire escape just outside the window of the apartment, down the side alley there. We might be able to get in that way."

Marco sighed. Ever since Park Side, fire escapes hadn't been his favorite thing in the world.

"Ok, I'll go to the alley between the buildings, they don't know what I look like."

"Wait!" she grabbed his arm. "You're just going to leave me here?"

The fear was back, stronger and coming off her in heady waves. Marco took a deep breath, steadying himself in the face of it.

"I don't think we can get past them without one of them recognizing you," he said after a moment.

"No, I'm staying with you."

"Miss Moore—"

"If you leave me, they'll get me, I know it!" she said, her grip tightening on his arm, tears forming in her eyes. "I won't go back, you...you have no idea what they'll do to me."

Marco's heart constricted at the terror he felt from her.

"Alright," he said, patting her hand, "but they'll see you the minute we step off the curb so—"

Delilah dug in her pocket and produced a dark scarf, which she promptly tied over her hair.

"I have an idea," she said, taking his arm. "Do what I say, alright?"

"Depends."

Her demeanor changed in an instant. A wide smile on her face, flirtatious and adoring.

"Now, is that any way for a new husband to act with his wife? Here," she handed him a simple bouquet with a pale blue ribbon around it, "buy this."

"I don't think—"

"People are uncomfortable with public displays of affection, believe me, these men are not expecting me to be demonstrative."

Marco sighed and forked over some of his precious little cash to the eager clerk.

"Alright," she said, pressing herself to his side as they stood on the corner. "Cross quickly, like you can't wait to—"

"Got it," Marco said, not wanting Delilah to give him any reason to think about what she was about to say.

"If they look at us, kiss me like you mean it."

Marco nodded, a stiff smile on his face as they ran across the street.

"Don't look so terrified," she said, her lips near his ear like she was whispering sweet nothings.

"It's hard when I'm waiting to be attacked," he responded, through a wider smile.

They walked with what Marco hoped was the semblance of joy along the sidewalk to the steps leading up to the entrance to the apartment building. He could feel eyes on him, and a drop of cold sweat trickled down his spine.

Delilah giggled and pressed herself so tight against him that he could feel the shape of her body. Out of instinct, his hand strayed to her waist, just above her round hips and he held her tight. He was unused to the attention of a beautiful woman, that was usually Lionel's department. And, at this moment, it made him feel far too much on display.

They'd just begun climbing the steps to the front door of the apartment building and Marco thought they'd actually make it, when Delilah pulled his head down, her lips slamming into his.

It had been a very long time since Marco had kissed anyone, and it had been nothing to write home about. This, however, was definitely something.

Delilah's full lips were soft and open under his. Before he knew it, Marco was kissing her with fervor. His arm around her waist tightened, and he was surprised to feel genuine desire from Delilah, subtle and controlled though it was. He'd kept such a tight leash on his passions the past few years that it disarmed his internal guards in a moment to feel passion course through his veins.

He let himself sink into how Delilah felt in his arms, moving his lips against hers. Her tongue made languid exploration of his mouth and he gave a soft groan of pleasure. Marco realized with a distant shock that he was hungry for something, anything that didn't involve violence or secrets. The simplicity of a passionate kiss with a beautiful woman, even if it was in service to not getting killed, brought into stark clarity what he'd cut out of his life in service to others.

He would have taken the kiss deeper if she hadn't chosen that time to break it off. Her lips hovered so near to his that he could still feel the heat of them.

"Pick me up and carry me through the door," she said.

He swooped her up in his arms, planting a series of quick kisses on her lips, just to keep up the ruse, of course. She returned them with a hungry intensity he didn't expect. Low chuckles behind them punctuated the sound of his feet on the steps and the creak of the door as he opened it with some clumsiness.

"Second floor," she said.

Marco ran up the stairs with Delilah still in his arms.

She giggled on the first-floor landing. "You can put me down now."

"Oh," he set her on her feet, brushing hair back from his forehead and trying desperately to bring his feelings once again under control.

The mutual desire that had enveloped his senses only moments before was gone so suddenly that it was like someone had ripped a blanket off him on a cold morning. Delilah took a handkerchief from her coat pocket and wiped lipstick from his mouth, laughing again.

"Sorry about that," she said. "Though, I must say, you are not bad at it. You must kiss a lot of girls. I hope I rate well next to them."

Marco felt his face flush.

"No, I, uh, I don't…thanks, should we…?" He motioned up the stairs.

Delilah led the way to the second floor and down a narrow hallway. The last apartment had a neat mat outside with a red door that still smelled of fresh paint.

Delilah knocked twice, paused, then knocked three times, then once.

The door opened as wide as the chain would allow, a small sliver of a man's scruffy face peered out.

"It's us," she said. "Mr. Mayer and I."

The door slammed, followed by the sound of two deadbolts and the chain being unlocked. Then it was thrown open to reveal a man who would, under normal circumstances, be average in almost every way. His dark hair was shot through with gray, there were dark circles under his brown eyes and about two days of growth on his haggard cheeks. An expensive suit hung on his body in a dreadfully wrinkled state, the faintest glimmer of something like a chain hung around his neck, the end hidden from sight.

"What took you so long?" he asked once they were inside.

"It hasn't been all that long, calm yourself, Doctor."

"Are they out there?" he asked.

"Yes, so we need to leave out the fire escape," Marco said, taking a look out the window in the small living room.

"Are you insane?" Trace asked.

"It's perfectly safe," Delilah said.

Unless there's explosives inside the building and it's on fire, Marco thought with an internal wince.

"But what about…them?" Trace asked.

Delilah went to the tiny galley kitchen and rummaged in one of the drawers.

"Now is hardly the time to make a sandwich!" Trace said.

"Quite right," she said, returning and holding a strange-looking gun.

"What are you doing with one of those?" Trace asked.

"I stole it before the fire, thought it might come in handy."

"What is it?" Marco asked.

"A special tranquilizer gun, for those who are enhanced by artificial means or naturally powered."

Trace grunted. "Naturally powered, there's no such—"

"That will be enough," Delilah said.

Trace glared at her.

Marco could feel anger from Delilah like a sharp spike. But as quickly as it rose up it was gone, as if she tamped it down and forgot about it.

Once again, he was amazed by the control she had over her emotions and wondered if it was a product of what happened to her.

"Ready?" Marco asked, throwing open the window.

Something slammed into the door.

The three of them stared in shock, then Marco grabbed Trace's arm and pulled him to the window.

"Damn it, how did they know?" Delilah said, readying the odd-looking gun.

Another impact on the door produced a splintering crack. A third blow struck and this time the door gave, hanging off its hinges as one of the men from the street burst through the opening.

Marco pushed Trace through the window as Delilah aimed and shot without a moment's hesitation. The man went down like he'd run into a wall.

Delilah ran to the window while a second man came

through. Once she was out onto the fire escape, she shot again. It went wide. She shot once more and the man crumpled to the floor.

"Quick, before Six Man comes!" Delilah said.

"But—!" Trace said.

"No time, doctor!" Marco said, practically pushing the man down the fire escape.

The three of them sprinted down the rickety fire escape and made it halfway down the alley when six huge, identical men blocked their path.

"No, no!" Trace said, scrambling to a garbage bin and cowering.

"You are one naughty girl," all six men said at the same time.

"Original," Delilah said. "I have one shot left, who wants it?"

"Not I," they all said.

Marco tried to concentrate his senses, seeking out the original man. This was something he'd never had to do before, sift through pale imitations of feelings to find their source. It was disconcerting, like ghosts brushing up against his mind.

One of the copies lunged for Delilah, and she jumped out of the way, bringing her foot up into the copy's groin as she landed. The copy smirked and Marco began to understand.

Only the original will feel pain.

Delilah raked her fingernails down the copy's face and Marco grinned.

Mark the copies, smart woman.

Another copy threw a punch at Marco. He ducked under it and delivered a punch of his own to the copy's lower back. The copy didn't even wince. Marco reached down to grab a handful of dirty trash, smearing it on the copy's back, then punched him again. The force of

Marco's punch shoved the copy forward and onto his knees.

If the original feels pain, then he'd want to be out of the fight.

Quickly searching through the copies in front of him, Marco saw that one of them stood back a little, his muscled body tense with the desire to fight.

Marco was about to send his shadows to the one he thought was the original, but two of the copies stepped in front of him. One delivered a punch to Marco's face, which sent a bright flash of pain to his eye. The other punched his stomach, causing Marco to double over.

"Put me down!" Delilah screamed. "I'm not going back!"

Marco looked up to see one of the copies holding Delilah to his chest. She thrashed around, hitting and kicking as she struggled to get free.

Marco lunged from his crouched position and slammed his body into the copy holding Delilah. It dropped her as he and Marco fell to the wet, dirty alley.

"No one move," Delilah said.

Marco looked up and saw her face fierce and beautiful. In her hands was clutched a sharp piece of glass which she held just below her jawline.

"I'm not going back," she said. "I will die before I let you take me."

The six men laughed. "Dead or alive, that's the job."

Delilah pressed the glass harder into her skin, a garish line of red running down.

"But I'd bet," she said, "they'd prefer alive, wouldn't they?"

Marco stepped back a little. As much as his instinct told him to talk Delilah down, he knew that this was his only shot to get to the Six Man.

The speed with which his shadows flew from his body shocked Marco, as if they were wild animals too long kept in a cage. They wound around the Six Man, enveloping him in smoky darkness. Marco felt his vision go silvery gray, and in his mind, he ran through the door of the man's mind and straight to the rooms that held memories. Most people had a variety of colors to their memories, a stunning mixture of light and dark. But this man's memories were filled with twilight, the light ones weak and hard to grasp, as if the man himself couldn't even remember them.

Not for the first time, Marco wished he could manipulate the good memories, bring them out to the fore so this man could remember, just for a moment, what it was like to be surrounded by something good.

But I can't, so…

Marco grabbed one of the darker memories and threw open the door that led to it.

He could see a child, no more than eight, naked and shivering in a cell with concrete floors and bars all around. The child was sobbing, fear and pain vibrant in every sound.

"I can make it stop. You just have to do what I ask."

"I c-c-can't! Please d-d-don't make me…please, please…"

More pain lanced through the memory as freezing water was thrown on the child.

Marco gasped as he stepped out of the Six Man's mind to find the copies gone and the Six Man curled into a ball on the cement, sobbing like the child in the memory.

"You did it," Delilah said, smiling at him.

Marco stared at the Six Man. "Wha-what I saw…" He looked at Delilah, blood still trickling from the wound she'd inflicted on herself.

"How? How could anyone…?" he said, closing his eyes and willing the aftertaste of the memory to leave his mind.

"We have to go," Delilah said, shooting her last dart into the Six Man and quieting his cries, "before the others in the apartment wake up."

She was completely calm as she tied her scarf around her neck to stop the bleeding. Without a glance in the Six Man's direction, she collected a blubbering Dr. Trace and pulled him along. Marco tried to feel something from her, anything. It was like brushing up against glass. He knew there was something on the other side, but he couldn't touch it.

For the first time, Marco wondered how sane Delilah might be after years of similar treatment.

"Are you coming?" Delilah asked. "We will need to take a circuitous route back to your apartment to ensure no one is tailing us. We should start now."

Marco took one last look at the Six Man, those childish cries echoing in his mind.

"Right…" he said at last. "I'm coming."

The walk back to Marco's apartment was uneventful, though slow, since Dr. Trace saw possible assailants everywhere. When they finally walked into the chilly apartment, Dr. Trace fell onto the old couch in Marco's front room and asked for whiskey.

"Or whatever you've got," he said.

Marco shoved a sloppy pour of cheap whiskey into the man's hands, who drank it in one gulp.

"You're safe now," Marco said to him.

He laughed, and gave Marco a stark look. "You don't know what the hell you're talking about."

"He's right," Delilah said. "That's why we need to get out of Metro City. Doctor, when are we meeting the contacts?"

"I have it here."

Dr. Trace checked one pocket, then another. His eyes

grew large and he started digging in his pockets with quick, panicked movements.

"The papers with the location! The money!" he said.

"What about them?" Delilah asked.

"I-I…Oh god. I think in our haste to leave, I left them at the apartment."

"What? Why didn't you keep them on you?"

"I'm sorry," he said. "I should have, but I was…I don't know. I thought I at least had the train tickets in my pocket, I don't know what could've happened."

"Do you have any other money, anywhere?" Marco asked.

"No," Dr. Trace said, "my accounts are frozen, my apartment and bank are all under surveillance by now."

Marco sighed and looked at his desk. The manila envelope with the pictures he'd taken a few days ago sat there, a nice pay out guaranteed when he delivered them tomorrow. He had planned to use the money to fly back to Jet City, and give the information about the cure to Gerald.

There won't be any information to give if I can't get them to safety.

"I might be able to help," he said, "if you promise that you can deliver what I need."

"Dr. Trace," Delilah said, "the information, is it secured?"

"Yes, a locker at the train station," he said, producing a chain from around his neck, a key dangling from its end.

"Alright," Marco said, checking his watch. "I can get some money for you tomorrow. Can you figure out the rest?"

Delilah and Trace looked at each other, and then she nodded.

"I think there's another possibility, but…I'll have to check."

"Alright. Stay here, rest. I need to check on something.

Colleen might be back before me, let her in. You can trust her."

Delilah nodded.

"Dr. Trace," Delilah said, "you should sleep. We're safe here."

"You can use my bedroom," Marco said.

Trace nodded and stumbled into the bedroom, shutting the rickety door behind him.

"I don't think he's slept in months," Delilah said, shedding the bloody scarf around her neck. "I need to get cleaned up. I stashed some clothes in the empty apartment next door, I'll just get them."

Marco nodded and eyed the now-empty glass that Dr. Trace had left on the floor. It was tempting to pour one for himself, but he tried very hard not to drink while he was working, no matter how the case was going.

"Mr. Mayer?" said a soft voice just outside the open door.

"Henry," Marco said, smiling at the painfully thin man.

"Someone left this on your doorstep, but I thought it would get stolen, so I held onto it until you got back."

Henry held out a small bag with a drawstring tie. When Marco took it he could feel small, hard balls inside like...

Marbles? Did someone leave me a bag of marbles?

He opened it and took one out, a beautiful green and white glass marble.

The little boy in my dream...he was playing marbles...

"Pretty," Henry said, grinning.

"Yes," Marco said, putting the marble back. "Thanks, Henry."

"Sure. Well...guess I'll see ya around."

Marco smiled at the awkward man and watched him walk down the stairs. He glanced back once, dark eyes intense, as if he were trying to tell Marco something with a look. Marco was about to step out and make sure everything was all right, when Henry turned away and kept walking down the stairs.

When Henry was out of sight, Marco dug deeper into the bag and felt a small piece of paper inside. He pulled it out and felt his heart stop for a moment.

Liam, 4516 Starr Flag Avenue…That's what Brennan was trying to tell me. It is an address, but how is someone connecting it with my dreams? And why do I feel like I should recognize this address?

He didn't have a chance to think too long since Delilah returned at that moment with a very worn suitcase. He stuffed the bag of marbles into his coat pocket.

"You can clean up through there," Marco said, motioning to the tiny bathroom. "It's not much, but I keep it tidy. Towels are in the top drawer of the bedroom dresser."

Delilah nodded, her face tense, and took a step toward the bathroom, then paused. "Your power…what is it?"

He sighed. "I can see people's memories, their feelings, good and bad, but I can only manipulate the bad. I can make them feel the bad things. For most, it's like they're reliving memories or past fears."

"That's extraordinary," she breathed. "So, for Six Man you saw—"

"His memories of his time in the labs."

Delilah swallowed. "My god, that must've been…I'm sorry you saw that. I wouldn't wish that on anyone."

"Were all of you…tortured?" Marco asked.

"Those that didn't progress as the trainers wanted… or…" Her voice was low and hard. "Those that wanted to keep their conscience. They thought pain would be an excellent motivator. Both physical and…psychological. For some…those considered especially dangerous or uncontrollable…special collars were that dampened their powers and shocked them when necessary. Thankfully, I never gave them a reason to make me wear one…well, not until now, anyway."

Marco stepped toward her and reached a hesitant hand out for hers. Considering the kisses they'd exchanged only an hour earlier, it was strange to still feel unsure with her.

"I'm sorry," he said.

She looked up with a sad smile on her lips. "Thank you."

"Did you ever have a friend or someone who you trusted?"

"Once, but I learned the hard way never do that again."

Marco squeezed her hand. "That's…I'm so sorry."

She reached up and touched his cheek, running her fingertips down his short beard.

"Thank you. But you don't need to feel sorry for me."

The memory of their kisses came sharp and clear to Marco's mind and he stepped back. Though Delilah was beautiful and stirred him in a way no one had since Alice, she was also a client. There was a line in Marco's mind about that, and he wasn't going to cross it.

"I should let you get cleaned up," he said, putting his hand in his coat pocket. "And I need to check on something."

She nodded and went into the bathroom, leaving him with the haunting memories of the Six Man and an awakened desire that he didn't want.

CHAPTER EIGHT

The public library was a massive building with marble lions out front and steps that made one feel as if they were climbing toward a Grecian temple. When Marco stepped inside, the musty scent of books tickled his nose and he grinned. In the entire city, this was his favorite place, and he often went in the evening, staying until they kicked him out. He'd never been there in the late morning, like he was now, and was a little surprised to see so many people streaming in and out.

Unfortunately, he wasn't there to sink into one of the many large leather chairs and get lost in a good book. Instead, he took the elevator down to the basement, where the public records were kept. He wanted to look up the address from the mystery scrap of paper and see what significance the building might have before he checked it out.

It took a little digging, but Marco finally found a series of micro-fiche newspaper articles about the Chester Gardens apartment building at 4516 Starr Flag Avenue. As he read, the feeling that he already knew the tragic story of the building grew until his mind burned with it.

The man who managed the apartments had been killed in a car crash, leaving two sons. The youngest one died a week later, when he fell off the roof of the building and the oldest went missing soon after. Marco hunted for a photo of the children, and finally found one. Small and blurry though it was, he felt his blood run cold when he recognized the oldest son.

"He's the child in my dreams," Marco said, running a hand over his face. "How...? Why would he be in my dreams? What does this have to do with Dr. Brennan... unless...no...no, that's—"

Marco searched through other newspapers, ones with less than sterling reputations that would print more sensational versions of events. After an hour, he found what he was looking for; a small article from a rag of a newspaper, the micro-fiche damaged so that only the first paragraph was clear.

"Child's death the fault of supernatural influence," Marco read. "The tragic death of Malcom Strong is being linked with mysterious reports from other children of an unseen force that takes control of others and makes them do it's bidding. Children in the Chester Garden apartment building have reported being forced to steal, hurt themselves, and sometimes, others against their will. Could the tragic death of Malcom Strong be the result of a ghost haunting the building?"

Marco sat back, his gaze darting from the text on the screen to the floor.

"A powered child," he whispered. "That has to be it. But...what does it have to do with me?"

He searched through a few more micro-fiches and found nothing. The desire to go on, to dig deeper pulled at him. When he stood up to see if there were more articles or records about the building, he was rocked back by a sudden pain between his eyes.

Through the years, he'd gotten plenty of headaches from using his powers or reading late into the night, but none had ever felt so sharp as the one that now lanced through his head.

"I must be more tired than I thought," he said, rubbing his eyes. "I'm not going to find out anything else now. There'll be time to solve this after I get Delilah and Dr. Trace to safety."

He wrote down what little he'd learned as his head throbbed and put the paper in his coat with the bag of marbles, which now felt heavier in his pocket.

Colleen knew that Delilah Moore was the best lead she'd had in months to finding out what could have happened to her brother. She had no idea when Delilah would be leaving, and hoped it wasn't today. It would take a little time to make the woman talk. Time Colleen might not have.

Her long legs made short work of the distance from High Tide, and she had just pushed the door to the apartment open when something hard landed on her shoulders.

"Oh my god!" said Delilah. "I didn't know it was you!"

Colleen rubbed her shoulder and looked at Delilah, who was holding a toilet plunger like a bat. "No damage done, although you might want to put that down and wash your hands."

Delilah looked at the plunger and blushed.

"Yes, you're probably right," she said, going into the bathroom.

"You expecting someone in need of a good beating?" Colleen asked when Delilah had come out.

"We were attacked earlier. Can't be too careful."

Colleen nodded and asked, "When are you leaving?"

"Hopefully tomorrow, but…well, nothing seems to be going to plan, so who knows?"

"And then what? You've never said where you're going."

Delilah's smile became tight. "Why do you need to know?"

Colleen felt a pang of sympathy as she looked at Delilah's carefully guarded body language. She understood her hesitancy and fear better than most.

"I'm sorry," Colleen said, hanging her coat on a nearby peg, "I don't mean to pry. I just…if this organization is as powerful as you say it is, then they won't stop looking for you."

Delilah swallowed. "That's true. But…there are places where others have gone."

"So, safety in numbers."

"Something like that."

Colleen nodded. "Can I ask you something?"

"If you pour me a drink," Delilah said with a dimpled grin.

Colleen felt a jolt of surprise run through her.

Is she flirting with me?

She laughed, trying to make it sound cheerful, but it came out nervous. It wasn't easy to know when someone was flirting or being friendly. She'd misread the signs a few times and had ruined more than one friendship.

Delilah's eyes held hers, a spark of playfulness lighting them up.

Colleen turned away and walked the few feet into the galley kitchen. She wouldn't take a chance with Delilah, even if a fling with a beautiful woman might be fun.

No, I have to get her to tell me about Lumis. I have to save Andrew.

"I think the only thing Mr. Mayer has is cheap whiskey," Colleen said, pouring it into a glass.

"Anything right now would be fine."

Colleen handed her the drink and motioned for Delilah to sit in one of the chairs in front of the desk.

"I am sorry about your brother," Delilah said. "It must be hard to hear such news."

"Yes, but I have reason to believe that he might not be dead after all."

"Doesn't really matter, trust me. If he's been taken…"

Colleen leaned forward. "Tell me about Lumis, please?"

Delilah studied Colleen for a moment and set her glass on the desk.

"You want to try and save him, is that it?"

Colleen nodded.

"Walk away, Colleen," she whispered. "Trust me."

"He's my brother, I can't leave him with people like… well, however they are, it can't be good."

Delilah didn't say anything for a moment, her gaze far away.

"Just tell me how you got out. It might help me see a way in. Or just talk about the layout of the underground lab…anything might help," Colleen said, trying to keep her voice as gentle as possible.

"And if I do, and you get captured, what then?"

Colleen sighed and was about to press a little more when Delilah turned her head toward the door.

"Do you hear—"

Something hard hit the door at the same time something else came through the window, landing under the desk. Smoke began to fill the room and both Delilah and Colleen jumped up, covering their mouths.

The bedroom door opened and out came a disheveled and panic-stricken Dr. Trace.

Delilah tossed him a scarf, which he placed around his face, and Colleen ran to the door. Even though there was likely to be a further threat behind it, she jerked it open anyway, and then immediately ducked under a meaty fist.

Though it had been many years since she'd been forced to employ the fight training Grandfather had forced upon her, the muscle memory came back without hesitation.

Colleen delivered a blow to the man's diaphragm, then stood and punched him again across the face. He stumbled back into the two men behind him.

Smoke began to flow from the inside of the apartment, where two more men had climbed up the side of the building and through the broken window.

"Out!" Colleen shouted.

Dr. Trace ran past her and was immediately punched by one of the assailants in the hallway. Delilah raced out of the apartment and charged the man attacking Dr. Trace, a small, bright knife in her hand. She slashed the man's arm and took a slap to the face when he reacted.

Colleen turned so that her back was to the other apartment doors in the hallway, giving her ample room to maneuver as the four men advanced on her.

She could feel heat flow through her veins, like molten blood. If she let the power seep far enough into her hands, every touch would be agony to the attackers. It was a tempting solution to the current problem.

One of the men delivered a harsh punch across her face, pain shooting across her cheeks. He tried to follow it up with a punch to the gut but Colleen pivoted and punched him in the kidneys instead.

A sharp scream echoed in the hall, and Colleen could see Delilah stabbing the man who'd slapped her. He clutched his stomach and cried out as she drove the knife into his back twice.

For a moment, Colleen was mesmerized by the gruesome sight of this beautiful woman with blood splatter on her face and hands, a distant vicious gleam in her eyes.

It was enough for two of the men to get the advantage on Colleen. Their punches landed on her face and stomach with enough force to drive her to her knees, where they kicked her in the gut.

She rolled over, gasping.

As one of the men kicked her, Colleen could no longer hold back the fierce power coursing through her. When the man tried to kick her again, she caught his ankle and let the heat flow from her fingertips. The man screamed as his foot began to smoke, the smell of burning flesh stinging Colleen's nostrils.

She let him go and stood up.

"She's one of them!" said one of the men.

"What's the bonus for two, I wonder," said another, drawing a strange-looking gun from his overcoat.

"No!" Delilah said, throwing her knife at the man.

It stuck in his bicep and he dropped the gun to the floor.

Colleen knew that there was only one way to take care of the remaining men quickly.

I haven't done that in years...I swore I wouldn't again but if I don't...

Colleen released the fire in her veins, the world turned bright and a small ball of fire appeared in her left hand. The three men who were left standing stared at her, terror in their eyes.

Usually, Colleen hated that look. Today, she didn't care.

"You want to burn?" she asked, advancing on them.

They stepped away, scrambling for the stairs and running down them.

That's when pain shot up Colleen's leg and she dropped the fire ball.

"You freak bitch!" said the man whose foot she'd burned.

He'd been laying on the ground and stabbed her calf with a thick needle filled with a light green solution.

Colleen let heat fill her hand once again and pressed it to the man's face, who screeched in pain and collapsed.

Smoke began filling the hall and Colleen saw with horror that her fireball had landed on the wooden floor boards in front of one of the apartment doors.

She tried to call the fire back, but could only make the flames lean toward her.

"What's…? I'm…" Colleen fell to her knees as the world around her spun.

People began to run out of their apartments, shouting and crying. Cool hands seized Colleen by the upper arms and shook her just a little. She looked up into Delilah's face, which was going in and out of focus.

"We have to go," Delilah said, her lip split, blood drying on her hands.

"No," Colleen said, reaching out to the flames that were spreading. "I…I can…"

"Not with what he shot you with," Delilah said, pulling Colleen up. "Soon you might not be able to walk, we have to move!"

Colleen stumbled to her feet and half ran, half fell down the three flights of stairs. By the time they'd made it outside to the sidewalk, where the other residents of the building were huddled in the freezing air, Colleen could barely stand. She plopped down onto the slick sidewalk. Snow that would usually melt at her touch remained cold, as if she had no powers.

Smoke and small tongues of fire started spewing out of the windows. Colleen was conscious enough to feel an acute guilt pierce her heart as she looked around at the people whose home was now burning. She buried her face in her hands and let tears trickle from between her lashes.

A soft hand fell on her shoulder.

"Don't…" Delilah whispered. "You didn't mean for this to happen. "

"But it did," Colleen said, not looking up.

"You saved us, that's what you should be thinking about."

"But at what cost?"

"There are always casualties in a war."

Delilah's voice was so clinical, that it shocked Colleen enough to look up. Delilah held her gaze, face hard.

I've seen that look before, staring back at me in the mirror, and in the faces of Grandfather's best men.

Colleen squeezed Delilah's hand. She knew what took the warmth out of a soul and for the first time in a while, felt a kinship with someone. Even if it was rooted in the darker parts of herself.

CHAPTER NINE

Marco had hoped walking back to his apartment in the cold would clear his mind, maybe help with the headache that was now pounding behind his eyes. Instead, his mind worked the mystery of the powered child and Dr. Brennan's murder like a dog with a bone. The more he tried to think about it, the more his head hurt. And when he tried to distract himself, his thoughts always led him back to the articles he'd read, the dreams he couldn't shake.

Was the child in the articles and the powered person that had likely killed Dr. Brennan connected, or maybe the same person? Was the work Dr. Brennan had been doing before he met Marco part of all this? Instinct told Marco that the answer to these questions was likely yes, but he didn't have enough information to know for certain.

And then there was the matter of Delilah showing up on his doorstep. Delilah, who had been experimented on by men just like Dr. Brennan and who had confirmed Marco's fear that powered people were being made into weapons.

Powered children, to be exact.

The thought made his shadows itch as anger rose up in him. The kind of people who wouldn't blink at torturing children and making them into living weapons…those were very dangerous people indeed.

As he thought of all this, Marco felt like he could see a hint of connection.

Like a face that you can't quite place, even though it's on the tip of your brain…powered children being experimented on… powered child at the apartment—

He gasped as pain sliced through his mind. It was so sudden and sharp that he had to lean against a nearby building until it eased.

I must need more sleep or…

Looking across the street, he saw the dingy liquor store that carried cheap, though not entirely disgusting, whiskey.

With the way Dr. Trace was drinking when I left we might need more…and a drink might help ease this pain.

After a few more minutes of deep breaths and waiting for the last dregs of blinding pain to ease into a terrible ache, Marco walked across the street to the store. It was busy as usual, the people around him oozed loneliness, depression, and more than a few alcoholic cravings. The emotions slithered over his consciousness, leaving their oily stain behind. Marco threw some money on the counter and didn't pay attention to the change the checker gave him.

Maybe it was the fatigue, or maybe it was the pain in his head, but the emotions were hard to shut out. The shadows under his skin were more active than usual and Marco could swear the tips of his fingers began to seep shadows for a moment.

Stop it! Get a grip!

He slowed his pace and measured his breathing. Once again, he imagined his mind like a house, and swept it as clean as he could.

That's better.

A fire truck zoomed past Marco, sirens blaring, and it startled him. Another followed close on the heels of the first, and the smell of smoke met Marco's nostrils. He looked at where the trucks were headed and his gut dropped to his toes.

Pushing past the remains of the headache, Marco ran the last block to his apartment. Smoke and flames were spilling out of the windows of the floor he lived on. The residents were huddled on the sidewalk, clutching each other or coats they'd been able to grab last minute. Little children cried or stared in awe at their home being consumed by the flames, while the adults shed silent tears. There was a growing group of people from the nearby buildings as well. Some brought blankets to wrap around those who hadn't the chance to grab a coat, others just gawked.

Some of the fire fighters were starting to connect their hose to the hydrant, while others were moving the crowd back and away from the building.

"Colleen! Delilah!" he shouted, moving around the fire-fighters. "Colleen! Dr. Trace!"

"Here!" called Delilah.

Marco shoved his way past more people and saw Colleen, Delilah and Dr. Trace huddled together, a little apart from the crowd. Silent tears made tracks down Colleen's face as she stared at the sidewalk.

"Are you okay?" Marco asked them.

"For the most part," Delilah said.

Marco reached out and touched her split lip before he could stop himself. She took his fingers gently off her face and smiled at him.

"It's all my fault," Collen said, her voice hoarse.

"She saved our lives," Delilah said. "Without her, Dr. Trace and I would be captured."

Colleen shook her head. "I shouldn't have done it like that."

Marco squatted down in front of her and took her hand in his.

"Believe me when I say that I know a thing or two about guilt," Marco said, his voice soft, "especially when it comes to 'gifts'. I'm sure you didn't do this on purpose."

"Doesn't matter," Colleen looked up at him. "I swore I'd never use it like that again. Now look…I lost control, and…"

Marco sighed, remembering the day at Park Side when he'd almost let the full depth of his power loose. It had felt good to go that far, which made him also feel like a monster. He'd spent many days wondering if he should use his powers at all after that.

Some days I still do. Oh…oh no!

"The pictures," he said. "The pictures for Mr. Banks were in there and now…damn it!"

"Is that really important right now?" Colleen asked.

"I needed that money for…" Marco motioned to Dr. Trace and Delilah. "What am I going to do now?"

"We'll think of something," Delilah said, though her voice trembled.

"We can't stay here," Dr. Trace said, as the flames started to die down. "If they found us that easily, they'll be back."

"And in the chaos of the fire, we'll be easy targets," Delilah said.

Marco ran a hand through his hair and wracked his brain for a place to take them. There was only one, but he loathed bringing Allegra into any of this.

Don't have much choice, and hopefully, it would be the last place they'd look.

"I know a place," he said. "But let's walk a block or two and get a cab, you all would freeze before we got there."

Marco tossed his trench coat over Delilah's shivering shoulders and they started walking away from the flames and the crowd.

"Mr. Mayer?" said a familiar voice behind him.

He turned to see Henry staring at him, gaunt face accented with soot, his thin body engulfed in a heavy blanket. Delilah stiffened just a little next to him, the barest hint of fear flowing from her.

"Henry," Marco said, "I'm so glad you're alright."

Henry nodded.

"Got out in the nick of time."

"Do you have someplace to go?"

"Sure, got family in the Irish quarter, Starr Flag. It's crowded, but they can put me up for a few nights, I hope."

Marco felt his mouth go dry at Henry's words.

"Starr Flag?" he asked.

"Yeah, you know it?"

"Sort of," Marco answered.

For a moment, Henry's bright eyes seemed to bore into Marco's, as if willing him to know something. Then the moment was over and Henry just stood there, grinning up at him.

"Well, hope you land on your feet," Henry said.

"You, too," Marco said.

An itch, small and almost imperceptible, went off under Marco's skin as he walked away. When he turned around, Henry was looking at him, a deep frown making the young man look years older.

As Delilah hailed a cab that stopped far quicker for her than they ever did for him, Marco took the slip of paper with the address on it out of his pocket and stared at it, willing the secrets someone was trying to tell him to be revealed. As if on cue, his head gave a sharp jolt of pain, and he rubbed his forehead.

"What's wrong?" Delilah asked from inside the cab.

"Hey buddy, you coming or what?" the cabbie asked.

"Yeah, I'm...nothing's wrong," Marco said, stuffing the paper into his pocket and squeezing into the front seat.

"Little Italy?" Colleen asked, as she paid the cabbie and got out.

"It's going to be okay," Marco said, as everyone else got out of the cab.

"Maybe I should've just gone back to my place," Colleen said.

"If those men survived, you now have a target on your back," Delilah said. "I'm sorry for that. Right now, you're safer with us."

"Maybe later, I can go back to your apartment and get some clothes and things for you," Marco offered.

"Why are we at a boxing gym?" Dr. Trace asked, looking up at the sign. "Surely we won't be staying here."

"There are apartments upstairs and I know the owner. Let's go around back."

It was late afternoon by now, and the streets were busy with people. Some of the shop owners Marco knew raised a hand in greeting, and then frowned at the odd, dirty collection of people he had with him.

Marco walked them around to the back door, an ancient and squeaky thing that was heavy and difficult to open. The backroom they stepped into was crowded with boxes and a newer washing machine and dryer, which was busy with a load of that day's towels.

"Wait here," Marco said, "I need to talk to Allegra."

He walked down a narrow hallway and into the locker room, Allegra's office to his left. She sat there, surrounded by her boxes and piles of papers, murmuring something to herself before looking up at him.

"Marco?" she said, getting up and coming to him. "What's wrong?"

"I have a favor to ask, and I'm sorry, Allegra, but I'm not

sure how much I can really tell you. It's part of a case and—"

"What do you need?"

His shoulders relaxed as relief coursed through him.

"A place to stay for one night, maybe two."

"You can have the upstairs apartment, it's furnished."

"It's not just me."

Allegra frowned and Marco led her into the backroom. She stopped short when she saw the assembled group, their clothes and faces bloody and soot covered.

She swore in Italian and looked at Marco.

"What is going on?"

"It's a long story."

Allegra eyed Colleen and Delilah, almost completely ignoring Dr. Trace, who glared at her with acute suspicion in his beady gaze.

"You trust them?" she asked after a moment.

"Yes," Marco said, "but...Allegra there are people looking for them and they're not pleasant. I just need a place to hide for a day or two, while I figure out what to do next."

She nodded. "Come with me, I'll give you the key."

Marco followed her to the office where she got a small key ring from her desk.

"Give this to them," Allegra said, "it's the first apartment. Not very big, but it will work I think. The other one is full of boxes, but I can have some of the boys move them tomorrow if you need the extra room. When you get them settled, you and I need to talk."

Marco nodded, his relief beginning to vanish. Once he'd delivered the key to Colleen and sat back down in Allegra's office he was feeling downright nervous.

She closed the door and sat down next to Marco instead of behind her desk.

"What kind of trouble are you in?" she asked.

"It's complicated."

She chewed the inside of her cheek, her gaze thoughtful. When she spoke next it was slow, measured.

"I know a thing or two about you, Marco. Things I'm sure you think are secret. I know things about other people too, about those two women, for instance."

It felt like a cold hand had gripped Marco's insides as he heard what Allegra was really saying.

"How?" he asked, voice hoarse.

"It is a gift. I look at someone and I see it, like an aura around them. First time I met you, I saw it."

"Do you know…what mine is?"

"I can tell how powerful a gift is, and by the color of the aura if it's mental or physical, but not the specifics, no. Your mother told me what your gift is, so I know more about you than most."

He looked down. "She was afraid of me."

"No," Allegra took his hands in hers and squeezed. "No sweet boy, never. She was afraid *for* you, but never of you. Before she died, she asked me to watch over you, to protect you from anyone who might want to hurt you because of what you were. I swore on the holy rosary to protect you with my last breath."

"Is that why Dad moved us so suddenly? Did something happen?"

She leaned back a little, studying him. "You don't remember?"

Marco shook his head. "That time just after she died, it's fuzzy in my memory. Some things are clear, others are… cloudy. Do you know what happened?"

Allegra took a deep breath. "Yes. Someone did threaten you, and I convinced your father to take you away from here."

"Who threatened me?"

"Doesn't matter, they didn't succeed."

"Allegra—"

"What does matter is that you stay safe. And that brings me to my next question: Whatever this case is, is it worth your life? Because from the look of things, this is dangerous and will only continue to be so."

"I just need to get Miss Moore and Dr. Trace to safety, then it will be done and I'll…I'll move on."

"I see. Go back to Jet City?"

"Maybe. I don't know. I just need to finish this."

"All right. I will help you. I know someone who might be able to get your friends to safety, across the border to Canada."

Marco frowned. "How would you know—"

"That's my business. Now, off you go. I need to make some phone calls."

CHAPTER TEN

Whatever the man had injected into Colleen didn't last very long, and by the time they'd pulled up to the boxing gym, she felt clear-headed enough to slip out the back door while no one was looking. She walked with speed out of Little Italy toward her apartment, hoping no one would worry too much about her absence.

She didn't want Marco poking around her apartment and seeing anything of her past. Those were her secrets and she would decide when and if anyone found them out. With only one block left to go, Colleen started to relax.

That's when a black car cut her off just as she was about to step off a curb. Her stomach dropped and she felt her entire body go hot. She recognized that car.

The driver stepped out, a mammoth of a man with a cold stare.

"Grandfather would like a word," he said, his voice like the boom of a cannon.

Colleen swallowed.

She could run, but chances were good that Grandfather had men all over the block in case of something like that.

I could burn the son of a bitch.

The thought both shocked and appealed to Colleen.

Before she could decide on what to do, the passenger door closest to her opened and out poured a gravelly, annoyed voice.

"Get in the damn car, Colleen."

Her body moved to obey the command, a habit born of a lifetime of learning that it was painful to resist.

Inside, the car was warm and smelled of cigars and something medicinal that Colleen couldn't place. The buttery red leather cradled her body as she sat, keeping as much space as possible between herself and the man next to her.

What most people were surprised to learn when they met Grandfather Malone was that he was short, but also built like a small tank. Or at least he had been the last time Colleen had seen him.

He had a dark blanket over his legs, and a thick scarf wrapped around his neck, as if he were freezing. His usually full face was sunken, like a deflated balloon, with glassy eyes narrowed under bushy eyebrows. The coat he wore, which he used to fill out, now swallowed him in folds of fabric that hung unnaturally on his thin frame.

I had heard he was sick but...good lord!

She didn't want to stare, but shock must've shown on her face because Grandfather scowled at her.

"Thought you could hide from me, did you?" he said, his voice the only thing that hadn't changed. Colleen didn't answer. The truth would earn her slap across the face, which she was willing to bet would still hurt in spite of his loss of muscle mass. "Doesn't matter," he continued. "I found you. Working for some wop no less. Have you no pride?"

Again, she said nothing.

Grandfather harrumphed, and then coughed, a wet

phlegmy sound that made Colleen wince. "You're lucky I find your situation advantageous."

"How?" she asked before she could stop herself. He'd poisoned every friendship she'd ever had and she'd be damned if she'd let him do that now.

"Oh, you're speaking now?" he coughed again, wiping his mouth with a white hankie. "Your brother made a rather interesting discovery before he disappeared inside Lumis Chemical. Can you guess what it is?"

She shook her head, stomach flipping to hear him speak about Andrew.

"In the basement, they were doing experiments. Experiments to develop super powers in people. Andrew insisted he could get me files, scientific formulas. Just after he disappeared, I sent in a couple of my best men to see what they could find. And turns out, Andrew was right."

"What does this have to do with me?"

"Word is that Lumis burning was no accident, that it was set by two people who escaped: a doctor and a super-powered whore that goes by the name of Delilah."

Colleen felt her body tense at his words and tried to keep her face neutral.

"From what I hear, they are your boss's new clients. One of them took some files that I want, and you're going to get them."

"How?"

"Figure it out! Look for an opportunity, a weakness. Have you forgotten everything I taught you?"

He tapped his driver on the shoulder and the man passed Grandfather a manila file folder.

"Before you get out," Grandfather said, tossing the folder into Colleen's lap. "In case you decide to double cross me, I thought you should know the consequences."

Colleen felt her throat tighten as she opened it.

There, on the very top, was a photograph of the only woman she'd ever loved.

Karen had changed very little from the last time Colleen had seen her. In this picture, she was in a blue evening gown that made her pale skin glow and her blue eyes stand out in her oval face, her now long red hair was swept up on top of her head. She was standing beside a tall man with dark hair and eyes, both of them were smiling.

Colleen just barely resisted the urge to run her fore-finger over the image.

Oh god how I've missed her!

"An engagement photo," Grandfather said, humor in his voice. "She's moved on. But I'm guessing by the look on your face that you're still caught up in your perversion."

"We had a deal," Collen said, her voice harsh with anger. "I come back and you leave her the hell alone."

"You didn't come back!"

"I left college."

"But you didn't come back, did you? No, you hid some-place until that useless brother of yours went missing. So, I've kept up on your pretty little girlfriend. She's done quite well for herself. About to marry into a family with deep pockets and political connections. It would be a shame if something happened just before the wedding, don't you think?"

Colleen met the old man's eyes, and hoped he saw the rage blazing in hers.

He could do it, no matter where Karen was living these days. Grandfather's reach extended beyond High Tide, with people in many cities owing him favors or who wanted Grandfather to owe them one. Karen could die and Grandfather's men would never even have to leave Metro City.

"I'll kill him," he continued. "While she watches. And

just before she dies, I'll make sure she knows to whom she owes all of it. Do we have an understanding?"

"Yes," she said, the word bitter in her mouth.

"Good."

———

She wanted to run out of the old man's car, but refused to give him the satisfaction of knowing just how rattled he'd made her. Still, she made short work of the last block to her apartment and took the stairs two at a time.

The minute the apartment door closed behind her, Colleen started shoving clothes into a large linen bag that she'd used on holiday weekends in England. She had no idea if or when she'd be back. The thought of leaving the few precious things she'd acquired while building a new life made her stomach clench. Especially the photo album she kept hidden in the floorboards of her living room.

There's one picture I'm not leaving behind.

She hurriedly popped the floorboard up and flipped to the page with the photograph that was her favorite. A sunny afternoon in spring, a red-haired woman with freckles and bright blue eyes, laughing. Colleen could almost hear Karen's laugh whenever she looked at the picture. Just after this image had been captured, they had shared a first kiss, and Colleen had thought she'd never want to kiss anyone else again.

Using her fingernails, Colleen pried the photo out of its place and pressed it into a book of poetry, then shoved it to the bottom of the bag. She put all her toiletries into a smaller bag, and grabbed an extra coat and scarf for Delilah. The bag was heavy by now, but not so much that Colleen couldn't carry it.

The last thing she did was go to a false bottom she'd built into one of the drawers in her dresser. Popping the bottom open she pulled out several hundred dollars in cash, along with an old passport she'd used when Tina had sent her Cambridge. These she stuffed into a pair of dark tights, rolled them up and stored them with the book of poetry at the bottom of the bag.

Colleen indulged in one last look around her home. The dark orange and red walls, the art she'd painstakingly collected over the years, her lush house plants, the old and new books on their repainted bookshelves.

"I did it once, I can do it again."

And with a deep breath, she pulled the door open and walked out.

———

Marco climbed the clean, well-maintained stairs to the one-bedroom apartment above the boxing gym. The door had been painted recently and gave barely a squeak of protest when he opened it and stepped into a small little entryway of sorts with hooks on the wall for coats and hats. The entryway opened into a wide room with a large window at the far end. It looked out on the cafes and bakeries across from the gym and let in an abundance of afternoon sunshine. Under the window sat a comfortable couch and chair. A low coffee table squatted in front of them. Against the wall to the left sat a small stereo and record player, against the opposite wall was a small, empty bookshelf. It made Marco think of the books that had been in his apartment, which brought the picture of Alice to mind. For the first time since seeing his apartment building ablaze, he felt a pang of loss. The photograph and books had been the only things Marco had cared about in that place. The books could be replaced, but not the picture of Alice.

Maybe it's for the best. The sooner I move on…And I'll need to go to the meeting with Mr. Banks tomorrow empty-handed. God, he'll be steamed about the pictures.

Marco grinned at the thought of pissing off the vulgar man.

Let him hire someone else to take dirty pictures. I'm done with it.

As he walked further into the room, his shoes sank into a new area rug that sat on top of a worn, but freshly-stained hard wood floor. To the left of the couch was a small dining area, with a table and chairs that just barely fit in the small space. A galley style kitchen was just off the dining room, with a small window above the sink framed with green-and-white checked curtains that reminded Marco of the house he'd grown up in.

A modest-sized bedroom opened off the main room to his right and from it Delilah came, looking as if she'd just washed her face and brushed her hair. Though her clothes were still stained with soot and blood, and her smile was anxious, the late afternoon winter sunlight filtered in and lit the golden undertones of her skin and hair.

Marco tried not to stare, tried even harder not to feel anything. Both were a losing battle.

Another door next to the bedroom opened, revealing a tiny bathroom. Dr. Trace stepped from the room in clean clothes that were a tad large on him.

"Anything to drink in this place?" he asked.

"Check the kitchen," Marco answered, glancing into the bedroom. "Where's Colleen?"

Delilah looked around, eyes wide. "I thought she was with you."

"Damn it! She can't just go walking around with those people out there."

"You plan on locking her up for the rest of her life?"

"No, of course not, I just…Maybe I can get her to safety with you and Dr. Trace."

Delilah frowned and sat down on the couch, looking out the window.

"How do we get away now?" Delilah said. "They're probably watching the train station, and the buses."

"Allegra has someone who can help."

Delilah's gaze whipped around to him, eyes narrow. "How?"

Marco quickly explained what he knew.

"And you trust her?" Delilah asked.

"I don't have a reason not to."

"You didn't sense anything? With your powers?"

"I generally don't use them like that on people that I know."

"Why not? Wouldn't it make everything easier if you never had to doubt someone's sincerity?" she asked.

"Maybe, but it would also mean no one would really trust me. I don't want people afraid of me in that way."

"Then you have no idea what her real motives are in this."

Marco sat down next to her. "I trust Allegra. I've known her most of my life. If she says she knows someone who can help, she does."

Delilah started to say something, and then stopped herself. She gave Marco a little smile instead and nodded.

There was a knock on the door as Dr. Trace stepped out of the kitchen, a glass of amber liquid in his hand. Marco opened the door and Allegra stepped in. A faint whisper of nerves came off her and Marco had to stop himself from exploring it. He'd meant what he'd said to Delilah, but had to admit that sometimes it would be nice not to be taken by surprise.

"I called my contact," Allegra said.

"Contact with whom?" Dr. Trace asked, his eyes narrowing.

Allegra gave him a sharp look.

"Many years ago," she began, "a friend of mine realized the need for powered people to have a way of escaping, if their secrets were discovered and they were in danger. He formed a small underground group to get passports, money, and passage for powered people. He can get you to and across the Canadian border safely."

"When?" Marco asked.

"He'll be here in two days, three tops. It's the best he could do. You're welcome to stay here until then."

Marco looked at Dr. Trace, whose gaze had gone to the floor, and then at Delilah, who was looking at Allegra with a smile. "If Marco trusts you," she said. "Then, so do I."

Allegra gave a quick nod, then returned Delilah's smile. "Thank you. In the meantime, I'll go to the market and get some food, I'm sure you are all hungry."

"That's not necessary," Delilah said.

"It's my pleasure dear," Allegra said. "Marco would you come to my office and help me make a list?"

Marco nodded and followed her out.

When they were down the stairs, they walked through a door to the right that led into the storage room they'd first come through. Allegra led him to a far corner where some of his boxes were stored. Marco was grateful that he'd been too preoccupied to ever get them out of the storage room.

He helped Allegra lift the top two boxes off one of the stacks of boxes, his breath hitching when he saw which one she was opening.

"Allegra!"

"I apologize for being nosy," she said as she opened it. "Though to be honest, I already knew. Anyway, I thought you might need this."

She pulled his Shadow Master duster and mask from the bottom of the box and held it out to him.

"I couldn't find the rest," she said.

"I'm wearing the chest piece and the rest was in the apartment."

Marco took the pieces, staring at them as memories flooded his mind. He had to take a deep breath to push them all away.

"I never wanted to bring this part of my life out here," Marco said.

"Why not?"

Marco paused. "It was too wrapped up in Steel and Serpent."

"Those we love return to us eventually," she said, patting his arm. "But for now, these people need you. And I think you need this."

He picked up the mask from the top of the suit.

"They already know about me," he said. "I don't think a mask is going to be needed."

"No...however..." Allegra went back to the box and pulled out his spare shoulder holster and grappling gun. "...this might be useful."

He smiled in spite of himself as she placed the holster on top of the duster.

"I was hoping this job would be straightforward."

"Few things in life are," she said, straightening and smiling at him. "Now, help me plan dinner. It's been a while since I've cooked for anyone but myself and the occasional gentleman caller."

CHAPTER ELEVEN

Colleen had taken a circuitous route back to the boxing gym, hoping to lose anyone that Grandfather might have following her. Just before she crossed the street to the gym, she could have sworn she saw someone, but when she turned around, no one was there.

She filed it away and let herself into the back door of the boxing gym.

"Are you sure you want to do this?" said a male voice.

"No, but what choice do I have?" said a woman that sounded like Allegra.

Colleen kept to the shadows, staying still as possible.

"I'm surprised Jake agreed to do this for you," the man replied.

"It's not for me. Jake's mission is to help powered people. If it was just me he'd tell me to jump in the river."

"He'd probably help you get there."

"He's helping Marco and the others."

There was a pause in the conversation.

"Have you told him…?" the man asked.

"No, not really. And I'd thank you to keep your mouth shut about it."

"You did it to protect him."

"Marco won't see it like that."

Colleen heard a rustle of clothing, perhaps the two speakers hugging.

"You want to come for dinner?" Allegra asked.

"No, Maggie's expecting me."

There was a wet smacking sound that Colleen was sure was some very enthusiastic kissing.

"I'll see you tomorrow," the man said.

"Good night," Allegra said.

Colleen stayed hidden in the shadows for a few minutes, considering her situation. There were too many secrets swirling around. Her secrets, Marco's, Delilah and Dr. Trace's, and now, Allegra's.

If we all get out of this alive, it will be a miracle.

When she was fairly certain she could act like nothing had happened, Colleen walked through the far door and up the stairs to the apartment. The smell of garlic, herbs and bread made her stomach rumble with hunger.

When she pushed open the door to the small apartment, Delilah turned from the table she was setting.

"You're back," she said, giving Colleen a bright smile. "We were starting to worry."

Colleen put her very full bag on a nearby couch. "Sorry, I had to get a few things." She held up the extra coat and scarf from the top of the bag and handed them to Delilah. "I thought you could use these. They'll be a little big, but…"

"Thank you, that was very thoughtful of you," Delilah said, giving Colleen's upper arm a squeeze before hanging the coat and scarf up in a nearby closet.

Marco came out of the kitchen to the left, a kitchen towel tied around his waist in place of an apron.

"Why didn't you let me go? Or at least wait for me?"

"I'm not helpless, in case you hadn't noticed," Colleen said.

"Of course not, you might have needed someone to watch your back though."

Colleen swallowed the lump of guilt welling up in her throat. She would have to betray him to do what Grandfather wanted, and then what?

Would they call me friend if they knew who I really was?

"Hey," Marco said, stepping toward her, concern etched on his long face. "You okay?"

"Sure, just...you know, I burnt down a building, men are after us. And I'm starved."

"Well, one of those things I can help with. The other... maybe we can work on your control...if you want."

Colleen's posture straightened, a familiar suspicion filling her mind. When she really looked into Marco's eyes, however, she could see his genuine concern, something she'd had so little experience with outside of Cambridge.

"Thank you," she said, her voice rough. "I'll think about it."

Marco's grin widened. "Dinner will be ready soon."

The door behind Colleen opened and in stepped Allegra. Colleen held her gaze for a moment, wishing she could see what secrets the woman was hiding.

Allegra paused and gave Colleen a warm smile. "I'm glad you're safe. Did you get what you needed?"

"Yes ma'am."

"Please, call me Allegra." She nodded in the direction of the small bedroom. "I believe Marco decreed that the women would have the bedroom tonight, and the men would take the sleeper sofa, if you'd like to put your things in there."

Colleen nodded, feeling Allegra's eyes on her back as she walked the few feet to the bedroom.

Dinner was simple and delicious. Colleen was surprised to discover that her boss was a good cook.

"I never saw you actually cook. I thought all those spices were for show," Colleen said, sipping a second glass of wine.

Marco wiped sauce from his lips. "I haven't really needed to cook. My aunts keep me well fed with leftovers and casseroles."

"But you're obviously very good at it," Delilah said, resting her chin on her hand and looking at Marco.

"Thank you," he said, giving Delilah a grin.

Colleen looked between the two of them and inwardly sighed. It didn't take a genius to see the growing attraction between them, or how uncomfortable it made Marco. She didn't understand why, he didn't seem to prefer men.

Though I'd bet it has something to do with the photo that's in his room...used to be in his room.

She cringed a little and took another sip of wine.

"You have an extraordinary gift," Dr. Trace said, his liquor infused breath making Colleen wince as he leaned toward her as if she were a curiosity. "When did you come by it?"

Colleen recoiled from him and didn't respond.

"Perhaps Colleen doesn't want to talk about it," Allegra said, as she began to clear the dishes.

"How would you know that? You have powers?" Dr. Trace demanded.

Allegra paused, just for a second, but it was enough for Colleen to notice.

"Dr. Trace," Delilah said, "I believe you've had too much to drink."

"And I believe you're not the boss of me! No one is anymore. Isn't that the point of this little escape?"

"Dr. Trace, maybe Delilah is right," Marco said.

He laughed. "Delilah now, is it? Not even her real name, if she ever had one."

"That's enough," Delilah said, her voice cold.

"Isn't it though? I can't wait to be rid of you and all these freaks! A normal life, is that too much to ask for?"

"I think Dr. Trace might benefit from a private room," Allegra said, coming out of the kitchen. "I have a cot downstairs."

"We're not getting out of here alive, you know that, right?" Dr. Trace said, not budging from his seat. "They'll find us, especially you. You're his favorite." He swung his gaze to Delilah, whose face flushed, a murderous glint in her eyes.

"Careful what you say," she whispered.

"Or what? You'll walk into my mind and drive me crazy like you did—"

With lightning reflexes, Delilah threw a steak knife at Dr. Trace, the tip sticking into the wooden back of the dining chair.

He plucked the knife from the chair and slammed it down on the table.

"You crazy bitch!"

"That's enough!" Marco said, getting to his feet. "You're drunk and need to sleep it off."

Dr. Trace held up his hands and glared at Marco. "Careful hero, I'm the one who's got what you want, not her. Or, maybe I'm wrong about that. She usually has something every man wants."

Colleen felt her powers begin to flow under her skin as anger sparked inside her. One look at Marco and Colleen knew that he was beginning to lose his temper, as well.

"That's enough," Allegra said, her voice low. "You will leave and go to the cot in the storage room."

Dr. Trace gave Marco and Delilah one last glare and

stood up, then stumbled a little on the way to the door and slammed it open.

"I'll get him a blanket, make sure he doesn't do anything stupid," Allegra said.

"Be careful," Marco said. "He may not have powers, but he's drunk and angry."

"Nothing I haven't handled before."

The heat under Colleen's skin still burned, but she controlled it. She didn't want to burn down two apartments in one day.

The three of them sat silently sipping their drinks.

"Maybe he's right," Delilah whispered. "We won't make it."

"Hey," Marco said, putting his hand over hers, "you've made it this far, he's just scared."

"He's not the only one."

"But look how far you've come," Colleen said. "And now you have new allies. It's hopeful."

Delilah gave Colleen a small smile. "Maybe."

"Why don't you get some sleep," Colleen said. "I'll start on the dishes."

"I'll help you," Marco said, giving Delilah's shoulder a squeeze before getting up.

The kitchen was just barely a separate room from the small dining area, but it was enough for Colleen to feel like she and Marco could talk in private.

"I'll wash," Marco said. "You rinse and dry?"

Colleen nodded.

The smell of cheap dish soap floated on the air, as the sink filled with hot water. Marco rolled up his sleeves, revealing hairy, muscled forearms, one with a jagged scar running down it. Colleen grabbed a large green dishtowel from a drawer and took the first plate Marco handed her.

At first, they were silent, each going about the task with a comfortable familiarity that made Colleen's stomach clench. How could she betray the first real friend she'd had in years? And yet, how could she let Karen die?

"That guy is piece of work," Marco said, as he passed her a soapy plate.

Colleen nodded.

"I hate to say it but I wish he'd just give me the key and go his own way."

Colleen dried the plate and realized one solution to her problem.

The key! If I can get the key from Trace, then Marco would get what he needs and Grandfather could have Trace.

Then she realized what would likely happen to Trace, the brutality Grandfather would subject him to in order to get what he wanted. What scared Colleen as much as Grandfather having powered people at his disposal, was that she wasn't sure she cared what happened to Trace.

He's a vile jerk, but does he really deserve that?

"Are you afraid? Of being found out, I mean," Marco asked.

Colleen jumped, startled out of her thoughts.

The soapy plate almost slipped from her fingers before she realized exactly what Marco was asking.

"My powers?"

He nodded.

"Yes," she swallowed, both relieved and disgusted that Marco was so easily deceived. "I guess that's it."

"Hiding for so long, and then being exposed like that, it must be hard and frightening."

She nodded.

"I'm here for you," he said, turning to face her. "You don't have to be afraid or feel alone. I'm your friend and I'll do what I can to help you."

Colleen looked away, hiding the tears that sprang to her eyes.

"Thank you," she whispered.

"I'm very sorry about your brother. That must be very hard."

"I don't think he is dead though."

"Oh? New information?"

"Something like that."

"You know, besides being a good cook, I'm not a bad private investigator. I could look into it for you."

She forced a smile. "Thank you, but I wouldn't want to put you in any danger."

Marco laughed. "I seem to find it no matter what I do."

"Yes, I guess that's true."

They smiled at each other, and Colleen wanted to scream from the guilt that shot through her. Marco was a true friend, kind and brave. He'd be there, right beside her, if she asked it.

And then he'd die, or worse. No, he needs to stay away from my family. I won't drag someone else into all this.

"Maybe a little music would help this go faster?" Marco asked.

Colleen nodded.

He went into the other room and clicked on the stereo. After a few moments, the sounds of The Shirelles drifted through the apartment. She let herself sink into the music, the smell of the soap, and the delusion of safety as Marco sauntered back into the kitchen.

CHAPTER TWELVE

With Dr. Trace downstairs, Marco had the sleeper sofa all to himself, but he couldn't sleep. The street lamps outside gave him just enough light to see the bottle of scotch and glass he sipped from. As his eyes adjusted, everything took on a pale, ghostly quality. He leaned back against the pillows, the cool air in the apartment tickling the hair on his bare chest. The mattress in the sleeper sofa was so thin it might as well have been non-existent. He could feel every spring and bar under him. But that wasn't what was keeping him awake.

The day's events whirled around in his mind, along with the questions his research had created, and the sudden loss of his apartment.

And then, there was Delilah.

He sighed and ran a hand through his hair. He couldn't shake the memory of their kisses, or how he felt. For too long he'd simply denied that part of himself, choosing instead a near monk-like existence. But why? What was the point?

As if summoned by his thoughts, the bedroom door

opened and out stepped the last person Marco wanted to see just then.

Delilah's hair fell over her shoulders in wavy golden strands, her curvy body was clad in a nightgown a size too big for her, and it hung off one shoulder. She looked disheveled and vulnerable, yet strong, as she held his gaze. She closed the door behind her and walked toward him.

"Is everything alright?" he asked, keeping his voice low.

She nodded. "I just can't sleep and I don't want to disturb Colleen. I thought...if you were awake maybe I could just...?"

He swallowed and motioned to the other side of the mattress.

The last thing Marco had expected was for her to climb under the covers and pull them up over her bare arms.

They stared at each other and Marco wished he had the guts to reach, just a little, into what Delilah was feeling.

"I hope this is okay?" she whispered.

"Sure," he answered, looking into his glass of scotch.

They were silent for a few minutes.

Delilah reached out of the covers and motioned toward the glass Marco still held.

"May I?"

He handed it to her and watched her sip the amber liquid.

"That's good," she said, handing it back to him. "Not too smoky."

"You know scotch?"

"Yes, I...yes."

Her face became tight and Marco thought about what her past must have been like. A beautiful woman, with powers that powerful men would want and how they might exploit them. He wanted to reach out and hold her, but feared what that might lead to. So instead, he offered the glass again, which she took.

"What Dr. Trace said tonight…" Marco began.

"I don't want to talk about it."

"I know, I just…" He turned toward her, but the mattress wasn't all that wide. Marco found himself closer to Delilah than before. He could smell the soap she'd used earlier that day, see specks of soot still in her hair. She put the glass on the floor and rolled toward him onto her side. He swallowed again and forced himself to focus on what he wanted to say to her.

"I wanted you to know that your past doesn't matter. Whatever they made you do, that's not who you have to be. You have a second chance."

Delilah's eyes became bright with tears and she shook her head.

"You are so…"

"What?"

"Different."

Marco couldn't help a grin. "Than who, or what?"

"Other men I've known. You're good, kind."

"I'm sorry I'm the first you've known like that."

Delilah smiled, her hand reaching out to touch the side of his face. "I'm not."

Marco didn't have to use his powers to see what she wanted in that moment.

"Delilah, you're my client," he said, taking her hand from his face. "I know we kissed before, and you're… you're beautiful, and in another circumstance…"

"But, you're afraid of abusing your position?"

"Yes."

Delilah smiled and bent closer until Marco could feel the feathery touch of her breath on his face.

"Is it abuse," she asked, "if I'm the one seducing you?"

Marco's mind went completely blank in that moment and she took the opportunity that silence afforded her and kissed him. She tasted like scotch and honey. Her body was soft and firm in all the right places as she pressed the length of it against his. His arms brought her tighter against him, spurred on by instinct and need.

In the back of Marco's mind, an image of Alice materialized, and he felt a jolt of guilt run through his body. His kiss faltered and Delilah leaned back just enough to look into his eyes.

"I'm not naive," she whispered. "This isn't love, it's what we both want and need. And that's enough for me."

Marco swallowed. Hadn't he just been thinking this afternoon about how much he needed to move on from Alice?

He pressed his lips to hers and all the emotions and desires he had caged for so long escaped. Delilah responded with equal passion, her nails digging into his bare back. Soon, she was biting his neck, as he practically tore her night gown off in his need to feel her body under his hands.

They were not gentle or slow with one another, as if they were both driven to expel the demons of their past in this one act of fevered passion. Delilah clung to him, pale legs wrapped around his waist, driving him on until they both could no longer hold on.

After, Marco held her against him, feeling her heartbeat slow, and her breathing even out. The sweat on their bodies quickly cooled and Delilah shivered in his arms. He pulled the covers over them, then propped himself up on one elbow, looking at her.

"Are you...?" Marco asked.

"I'm wonderful," Delilah said, stretching her arms overhead. "You?"

He smiled at her and smoothed back some of her hair. "Same."

She smiled and the dimple in her cheek appeared. Marco had wanted to kiss it since the first time he saw her.

Without over thinking it, he placed a light, breathy kiss to her cheek, then one on her lips.

Delilah's breath hitched.

"What's wrong?" Marco asked.

She was staring at him, a flash of sadness in her large eyes.

"Nothing, I just…nothing. Not one thing."

He caressed her cheek for a moment, and then took her in his arms. There was nothing he could say to wipe away her past, but perhaps tonight could be a new beginning for them both.

"We should sleep," she whispered, curling up within his arms. "Who knows what tomorrow might bring."

Marco nodded, and within a few breaths, he was out.

The dream felt far too real, and Marco couldn't find his way out of it.

He was in a basement apartment, at least that's what he thought it was from the dim lighting. Out of the darkness, the little boy from his dreams appeared, but where before, the boy had felt like an apparition, this time he was solid, real.

"Come on, let's go!" the boy said. "We have to leave! They'll be here soon!"

"Who?" Marco asked, his voice like it had been when he was a boy.

"You know who!" The boy's mouth was tight and his brows furrowed "Please, don't let them take me!"

"I won't."

Marco realized then that he was an observer this time. Off to the side he could see himself as a child, speaking to this person.

"We're friends," child Marco said, " I'll keep you safe. Use your powers with me."

"No! I can't!" the boy said. "You know what will happen, what happened last time. I won't do it again, I won't!"

"Alright, it's alright. I'll protect you, I promise."

The door to the apartment opened and in stepped Allegra, with Dante by her side. They looked younger, like when Marco's mother had died.

"I'm not going, you can't make me!" the boy said.

"You can't stay here," Allegra said. "Wouldn't you like a home, Liam? Someone to take care of you?"

The boy backed up, tears streaming down his face.

"He doesn't want to go," Marco said.

"I know," Allegra said. "But he doesn't have a choice."

She motioned for Dante, who stepped forward and grabbed hold of Liam, whose screams echoed sharp and primal in the basement.

"Stay away from him!" Marco yelled, his shadows shooting out of his hand and enveloping Allegra and Dante. The sounds of their screams pulled Marco from the dream and he shot up, drenched in sweat.

"What's wrong?" Delilah asked, looking around in a panic.

He shook his head, trying to dislodge the dream, which was starting to feel more like a memory now.

"I...just a dream," he said.

Delilah breathed out, shoulders sagging in relief. "Oh. Are you okay? Do you want to tell me about it?"

"Yes, I'm...I'm okay, but I don't want to talk about it. Thanks."

She planted a kiss on his cheek, a lingering one on his

lips, then lay back down. Marco followed, putting a hand on her round hip and trying to push the dream aside.

The harder he tried, though, the more it rolled around in his mind. Soon Marco found himself going over every detail. The dingy carpet in the apartment, the smell of cabbage and sausages. The way the boy looked. And...

Allegra said 'Liam'. That boy...I feel like I should know him. And that apartment...I would bet it's the one from the articles, on Starr Flagg. I need to go to that address tomorrow. I need to know what this all means. Allegra was so young, maybe it was from when my mother died?

He tried to focus on the last month or so of time after his mother's death, but the memories were dark and slippery. An acute sense of loss settled on Marco and he knew it had something to do with the child named Liam.

But what? Who is he?

He had a suspicion that somehow Allegra knew, and getting answers from her wasn't going to be easy.

After another half hour trying to go back to sleep, Marco gave up and got dressed.

Maybe a walk will help, some fresh air.

He got out of the apartment without waking Delilah and when he reached the end of the stairs, he took the door that led to the backroom of the gym. His duster was warmer than the trench coat, and if he was being honest with himself, Marco was tired of burying Shadow Master. It was a part of him that he was proud of, no matter how many bittersweet memories it brought up.

He had just walked through the door when he spotted Colleen, standing over a passed-out Dr. Trace. She was holding a chain with a key on it, and staring down at the drunk.

"Colleen? What are you doing?" he whispered.

She jumped, and spun around toward him, her eyes wide in shock. "I...I..."

Marco swallowed hard and stepped toward her. "You're taking the key? Why?"

Colleen held it out to him. "Take it, and let me have Dr. Trace."

He stared at her. "I don't...what's going on?"

"Damn it, Marco, take the key!" Her voice teetered on the edge of a whisper into a breathy screech.

Marco was never one to man-handle women, but as Dr. Trace stirred on his cot, he knew he had to get Colleen away from him. A few more seconds and he could have a fight on his hands that might cost him the information he needed.

Taking Colleen's arm, he pulled her through the back door and out into the frigid night. In spite of his duster, Marco felt the cold suck the heat from his body almost immediately. Colleen, he knew, wouldn't be the least affected.

"Now," he said, willing his teeth not to chatter, "what the hell is going on?"

Colleen started to pace, the key dangling from her hands. "It's not what you think."

"Oh really, and what's that?"

"I don't want Dr. Trace for myself. I...I need him to save someone's life."

"Who and what would he be able to do? Is this about your brother?"

"No, it's...Oh hell!"

She stopped pacing and looked down at the now thawed sidewalk. After taking a deep breath, she looked up at him and said, "Have you ever heard of Grandfather Malone?"

"Sure, what's that got to..."

Marco felt the air leave his lungs as a thought exploded in his mind.

Colleen nodded. "I'm his granddaughter."

He ran a hand over his face. "Oh my god."

"Yeah."

"Why didn't you tell me?"

"Because you'd look at me like you are right now! You'd never trust me, and rightly so!"

"Have you been working for him this whole time?"

"No. I ran away from my family, but they…Andrew's disappearance made me come back. I never wanted to be in the family business."

"So why now? And why Dr. Trace? Oh, wait…" Marco felt his face flush with anger as he realized the answer. "Grandfather Malone wants his very own powered goons, doesn't he?"

"Yes."

"You know—"

"He can't get that, yes! But this isn't that simple." Colleen's face crumpled and she turned away.

"What does he have on you?" Marco asked, forcing his voice into a softer tone.

It took her a moment, and when she spoke her voice was thick with grief. "A friend, one of the best I've ever had. And she will die unless I give him Dr. Trace."

Marco was about to say that she still should have told him, that no matter who it was, she couldn't do this, when Lionel's face shot through his mind. He sighed.

"I'm sorry."

Colleen's gaze swung up to his, and she frowned. "For what?"

"For… I don't know. For judging you, I guess. I would do the same if I were in your shoes. Hell," he said with a mirthless chuckle. "I am in your shoes."

"I know that your friend needs the information," Colleen said, holding the key out to him again, "that's why I was going to give you this."

Marco took the chain and stared at it. It weighed next to

nothing in his hand, and yet it was more precious than gold.

"Thank you," he said, tucking it into his pocket, "but I think I need to give this back to Dr. Trace before he finds out what happened. Don't need him getting spooked and running out."

"Dunno, that might be a win-win."

Marco stared at her for a moment, and then laughed. "I could see why you'd say that, but I gave him my word, just as much as I did Delilah."

Colleen's face softened with sadness. "You, Mr. Mayer, are a rare man. I'm sorry I betrayed you."

"You didn't, not really. You could've taken off with the key, you could've lied to me. You didn't."

"What now?"

Marco sighed, his breath coming out in a puff of steam. "Well, we need to figure out how to help your friend without giving Grandfather Malone what he wants."

"I shouldn't be surprised that you're willing to help me, but I am."

"Colleen, you're my friend. Of course, I'm going to help you."

She stared at him, fat tears falling down her round cheeks. "I...Thank you."

"You're welcome. Now," Marco shivered in spite of the warm duster, "can we go inside before I freeze?"

Colleen followed him in, and as the door closed, Marco turned to her. "How did you get this off him anyway? And how did I not see you leave the apartment?" he whispered.

"You were asleep. I...I sat down here for a while, trying to come up with something else that would keep my friend safe. When I couldn't, I slipped it off his neck...very carefully."

"He must be passed out cold. Hopefully he still is.

Oh…" Marco turned to her, his face flushing once again. "You've been awake all night?"

Colleen grinned. "Yeah, but don't worry. I didn't hear much."

"Listen I…She came out of the room and…umm…"

"I'm no prude, you don't have to justify it."

"I just don't want you thinking I'm taking advantage."

"Oh yes, Delilah is such a damsel in distress."

"Not what I meant."

"Stop worrying so much. You're the last guy I'd think would do anything like that. Just enjoy it. I mean…obviously, enjoy it, but…Can we stop talking about this now?"

"Yep."

Marco stopped her before they reached Dr. Trace's cot. "We won't let anything happen to your friend, I promise."

She nodded and carefully replaced the key around Trace's neck.

"Thanks."

CHAPTER THIRTEEN

The smell of coffee and fresh cinnamon rolls filled the air the next morning. Colleen heard Marco and Delilah laugh, and the oven door open and close. She was hungry, and a little uncomfortable at the thought of facing Marco after last night. But that was secondary to what had kept her from sleeping, even after she came back upstairs. She stared at the picture of Karen, trying to think of any way to keep her safe.

"There isn't one though," Colleen said to herself and closed her eyes. "I'll never be free of them, will I?"

A soft knock made her jump and she stuffed the picture inside the book of poetry on the night stand.

"Yes?" Colleen answered.

The door opened and Delilah peeked around it. "The first batch is out of the oven."

Colleen nodded. "Thanks, I'll be right out."

Delilah lingered at the door, biting her bottom lip.

"What?" Colleen asked.

"What are you going to do?"

Colleen paused, wondering if Marco had told Delilah what had happened.

"Are you coming with us, or staying here with Marco?" Delilah asked.

"Oh…I hadn't…I don't know."

"You'd be welcome, you know."

"Thanks, I appreciate it."

Delilah walked away, leaving the bedroom door open enough for Colleen to hear Dr. Trace's rough voice and Allegra telling him to not take it out on them if he had a hangover. Colleen indulged in one more look at Karen's picture before burying it in her bag. She took a deep breath and walked out into the living room.

Marco and Allegra were standing in the small dining room, their whispered conversation oozing tension and Colleen had a moment's panic wondering if Marco was telling Allegra about last night.

"I'm not sure what you're asking," Allegra said, as Colleen walked by toward the kitchen.

"Did I know someone at that time, who looked like that or went by that name? Was I friends with anyone?" Marco asked

"Is this really important right now?"

Colleen had only just met Allegra, but she could spot someone who was hiding something from a mile away. The conversation she had overheard last night came to mind and she eyed the older woman with renewed suspicion. Who was she, and what the hell was her angle here?

She busied herself with getting a cup of coffee, and then turned away from the two. There was no point in trying not to listen, the apartment was too small for that, but at the very least, she could give them the semblance of privacy.

"No, I guess not," Marco said, sighing. "I just feel like I know that boy, and I don't know how."

"Look," Allegra said, "after all this, we can talk more about this dream, alright?"

"Alright."

Out of the corner of her eye, Colleen saw Allegra walk away. She turned her focus back to the cinnamon roll on her plate. Marco came in and poured more coffee into his cup, his smile forced.

"Good morning," he said.

"Good morning," she said.

Colleen eyed the curious vest that peeked from the neck of the shirt Marco wore, and the grappling gun securely stowed in his shoulder holster. Colleen had seen these before, but had never asked about them. Then again, she hadn't realized she had been working with a powered person.

"What are you wearing?" she asked.

Marco took a long pull from his coffee cup before answering, his voice low.

"Well...I thought you'd have figured out who I am by now."

Colleen studied him a little more and shook her head.

"Ever hear of the Jet City Vigilantes?"

"What?" she breathed. "You're one of them?"

He nodded.

"Why aren't you masked?"

"What would be the point? You all know who I am."

"But everyone else doesn't."

"This is just for extra protection," he said, motioning to the vest. "I'm not looking to take that up again in Metro City."

Colleen tried not to stare at him but failed, her mind spinning as she tried to take in this new information.

Thank god Grandfather doesn't know!

Silence settled around them, uncomfortable at first, as they both chewed their cinnamon rolls and sipped coffee.

"About what I told you last night," Colleen said.

Marco's brown eyes held hers and he nodded.

"I have an idea, but I have to do it alone."

Marco opened his mouth, likely to protest, and Colleen held up her hand.

"I know I have no right to ask this," she said, "but I need you to trust me. Please? I have to do this alone."

He paused, brows furrowed. "You sure I can't help?"

"Positive."

"Alright. Will you need to leave this morning?"

"Probably not, why?"

"I have to go to Mr. Banks, tell him I don't have the pictures. And after that, I need to check on something, the sooner the better," Marco said, his voice low. "I'd feel better if you were here to watch over things."

"You expecting trouble today?"

"No. I'll just feel better with someone I trust here in case trouble comes."

Meaning he doesn't trust Allegra all of a sudden.

Colleen nodded

"Thanks." He smiled and put another cinnamon roll on his plate.

"You make these?" she asked.

"Yeah."

"Poor Delilah."

"What do you mean?"

"You're good looking, can cook and bake, and, from the smile on her face this morning, I'm guessing good in bed. She never had a chance, did she?"

Marco flushed a very deep shade of red.

"Then again," Colleen said, grinning. "Neither did you."

After breakfast, Marco left to do his errand, leaving Colleen to wonder what was so important. After checking the outside of the gym to make sure no one was watching them, and drawing some very curious stares in the process, Colleen had asked Allegra if she could use her office.

"I need to make a call and I need a little privacy," Colleen explained.

"Of course, dear," Allegra said, her smile a little too tight to be genuine. "Take your time, I've got some errands to run this morning, anyway."

Closing the door behind her, Colleen dialed the number and gave the coded message to the man who answered.

Less than five minutes later, the phone rang, and Colleen snatched up the receiver.

"What's wrong?" Tina asked without preamble or greeting.

"Grandfather...he knows."

Tina swore on the other end. "How much?"

"All of it, and then some."

Colleen quickly brought her mother up to speed on the situation. Tina interrupted to ask a few questions and interject some exasperated swear words.

"What do you need from me?" Tina asked.

Taking a deep breath, Colleen said, "I need help. I can't give Grandfather what he wants, you know that. But I can't let him hurt my friend, either."

Tina paused. "This friend...she was from college."

"Yes."

"I see."

Colleen waited, heart pounding in her chest. Her mother's tone made her wonder if she knew what Karen really meant to her, or if she was just wondering why Colleen would call in a favor for a woman she hadn't seen in years.

"I can help you," Tina finally said. Colleen let out a long breath in relief, but it was short-lived, "but you're not going to like the how. You going to be able to accept that?"

"I don't know, who are you going to hurt?"

"No one you care about."

The fact that she didn't deny that someone was going to get hurt gave Colleen pause.

"What are you going to do then?" she asked.

"Less you know the better. When it's done, though, you will come see me."

"Why?"

"Because you will owe me, that's why," Tina said, her voice hard. "This isn't charity. You ask a favor, you owe a favor in return."

Colleen swallowed the lump of panic in her throat, heat beginning to course through her veins.

"Alright," she said. "How will I know when it's done?"

"You'll know, and once it is, you come and meet me at my office."

Colleen dropped the receiver back in its cradle and stared at the phone. God only knew what she'd just agreed to, and what the price would be.

"But, Karen will be safe. And that's all that matters."

She wondered, as she left the small office, how many times she'd have to say that to herself to make it true.

Mr. Timothy Banks was a long time city councilman, export-import tycoon, and general rich ass. Marco would have much preferred to call him to say that the photos had been destroyed. Unfortunately, his address book had gone up in flames, as well.

At least I remember where he lives.

The tycoon had always refused to meet at the "grungy, toilet of a diner" where Marco usually did business. And, though it took some doing, Marco had managed to require Banks to pay the cab fare to his mansion an hour away.

He shifted on the worn leather seat as the address from the marble bag burned a hole in his pocket, and his mind kept going over his last dream. The connections were there, and Marco knew he should be able to see everything by now, yet there was still a mental block.

Like a wall I can't find the end of to get around. Why can't I figure this out? And what the hell does Allegra have to do with it all?

He sighed, the headache from the day before lingering behind his eyes.

And then there's Colleen being Grandfather Malone's grand-daughter…and then there's Delilah…Good god, last night…

Marco didn't know what he felt worse about. That he'd slept with Delilah or that he didn't feel more guilt about it.

What am I supposed to do, spend the rest of my life pining over Alice?

Part of him immediately answered 'yes'. The other part of him, the part that had given over completely to Delilah last night, knew that it was past time to let go of Alice.

And I can, once I get the cure for Lionel. I'm almost there. If I can just keep Delilah and Dr. Trace safe from…well, pretty much everyone.

Marco took a deep breath, preparing for Mr. Banks' legendary temper, as the cab pulled up to the ostentatious mansion.

A man in a dark suit jacket and tie came out one of the heavy, white-and-black doors.

"How much?" the man asked the cab driver, as Marco got out and walked toward the front doors. He didn't wait around to hear the amount or be escorted up the wide steps. The sooner Marco got this over with, the sooner he could get to doing what was really important.

A second man in a dark suit and tie met Marco inside the foyer and took his coat.

"Mr. Banks is waiting for you in his study."

"Thanks," Marco said, his worn shoes echoing on the black and white, marble tiled floor.

The hall felt never-ending and cavernous, with its vaulted ceiling and perfectly spaced paintings on the wall. Banks' wife, the one Marco had been sent to spy on, was a notorious art collector. He had to admit to a small amount of jealousy when he saw the scope and beauty of the pieces. He paused to take in a small but stunning painting by Van Gough, a twirling night scape that made Marco feel wistful and lonely.

How many times do they just walk past these, not even caring about the wealth of beauty around them?

"Sir?" said the butler ahead of him. "Mr. Banks does not like to be kept waiting."

Marco sighed and walked on until he was in front of a large white door. The butler was waiting at the door and knocked once Marco was close.

"Come in!" said a barking voice.

Marco stepped inside, startled by the difference, even though he'd been here several times before . Where the hall was cold in its starkness, the study was filled with warm browns and greens. A gleaming hardwood floor was covered with a thick rug in front of a large fireplace, where a cheerful blaze crackled and spat. Overstuffed leather chairs and a couch sat nearby, thick wooden end tables next to them. Green drapes were pulled back from two tall windows, letting in the light from the weak winter sun. A wide, long desk sat near one window, its surface crowded with papers, a large crystal ash tray at one corner.

The smell of cigars and brandy hung thick in the air, as did the taste of anger and fear coming from the corpulent man standing in front of the fire.

"Took you long enough," Mr. Banks said. "I gave you this job a week ago. Well? Where are my pictures?"

"There was a complication," Marco said, walking toward him.

"What would that be?"

"My apartment burned down, with the photos inside."

Mr. Banks just looked at Marco, puffing on his cigar. "So? Go take more. I know she'll be with that son of a bitch tonight. Go earn your fee."

The disdain and anger rolling off Mr. Banks as he looked at Marco was thick, putrid. Marco had to grit his teeth to keep it at bay, his shadows stirring with the effort.

"I'm sorry Mr. Banks, but the situation has changed. My equipment was also damaged. And, I'm on a new case that requires all my attention."

"You're welshing on me then? Is that it?" Mr. Banks laughed, a harsh, bitter sound. "I should've known better than to trust a wop!"

"No need to get nasty."

"I paid you a fee up front and I want my pictures!"

"That money's gone, it went toward the job."

"Which you didn't do!"

Marco took a deep, steadying breath. Whether it was the lack of sleep or the headache that refused to go away, he was having a harder than usual time keeping himself from being affected by Mr. Banks' emotions. And as a result, his shadows were starting to strain under his skin, demanding to be let loose.

"I did the job, sir. It was an unfortunate accident. I can give you the name of other private investigators, if you—"

Mr. Banks closed the distance between them. He was built like a tank with the face of a bulldog and the reputation as someone who didn't let anyone disobey him. When his face was inches from Marco's, he blew out a cloud of cigar smoke that made Marco cough.

"Listen here, you little shit," Mr. Banks said, "I hired

you and you'll do the job, or I'll make sure you're unable to do much of anything, ever again, you understand?"

"No."

"What did you say?"

"I'm leaving Metro City soon, I won't be taking any new cases."

"Is that right?"

Marco nodded.

Without preamble or warning, Mr. Banks back handed Marco across the face.

"Now, get to work. Before I have to find a way to motivate you."

The anger that overtook Marco was lightning fast.

He'd kept a tight rein on the fear and guilt over what he couldn't fix, the rage at a world where men and women filled with darkness got away with dark deeds. Day by day, month by month, he swallowed every insult men like Banks threw at him, told himself that it didn't matter.

But everything that had happened the last few days had eaten away at the inner walls keeping these feelings at bay. Banks was the last straw.

Before he could stop himself, shadows flew from Marco's hands and the world became silver and gray. The dark tendrils spun around Mr. Banks' body and face, leaving only the man's terrified eyes exposed.

"You will do nothing," Marco said, his voice as cold as the appearance of the world around him. "You will leave me and mine alone. You will find someone else to do your dirty work. You understand me, you waste of space?"

Mr. Banks gasped. "Wha…what are you?"

"A person who wants nothing to do with you anymore."

"N-no…you're…you're a freak!"

A word Marco had applied to himself on many occasions, and heard spouted from more than one mouth. Yet in this moment, when Mr. Banks was desperately trying to hold onto a shred of power, it set Marco's teeth on edge.

"Maybe," Marco felt the spot in Mr. Banks' mind to press and applied just a little pressure. "But I'm the freak who can make you—"

A wet stain spread across the front of Mr. Banks' pants.

"—do that."

Mr. Banks whimpered. "A-all right...all right! We're done, I swear it!"

Marco kept the shadows on him a little longer. He could see the house of Mr. Banks' mind, dark and menacing, yet also weak and sagging. He knew exactly where to push to make Mr. Banks incapable of doing anything to anyone ever again. It would be so easy, as it would have been so many other times. One less selfish man that abused the power he'd amassed.

And, like every other time before, Marco stopped just short of doing it.

Pulling back his shadows was harder than ever before, as if they had mind of their own and were determined to fulfill Marco's dark desire. When he finally brought them under control, cold sweat dripped down his body and he shook.

Mr. Banks fell to the floor, breathing in heaving gulps of air. Marco gave him one last look and turned to leave.

"You son of a bitch!" Mr. Banks said when Marco got to the door. "You better run, because when I find you—"

"You won't do a thing," Marco said, letting the shadows slip just a little past his fingers, just enough for Mr. Banks to see.

The man's eyes blazed, but he didn't say anything else.

Turning his back, Marco walked out. It wasn't until he was past the gates of Mr. Banks' property that he let himself fall to the ground, his body shaking uncontrollably.

He could count on one hand the number of times he had used his powers as he had on Banks.

Every time, he'd felt immediate guilt.

As he tried to get the trembling under control, it bothered him that this time – he didn't.

CHAPTER FOURTEEN

Marco couldn't sit outside Mr. Banks' property for long. The man was rightly enraged, and scaring him had only made everything worse.

Like poking a hornet's nest. What was I…? Doesn't matter. No time.

He forced himself to stand. The sweat on his skin brought a sharp chill from the cold air of the afternoon. The cab fare for getting back to the Irish quarter would be more than what he'd borrowed from Colleen earlier that morning, so Marco walked a good distance, hoping it would help to clear his mind. By the time he did hail a cab, he felt enough like himself enough to put on a good face. He was determined to focus on the task at hand, not what he'd just done.

It was time to get to Starr Flag Avenue and, hopefully, get some answers.

The cab dropped him a few blocks away. He walked the rest of the way through the well swept streets, past shops that were prosperous and full of customers. He turned down a narrow one-way street, and then another, finding himself in the backend of the Irish Quarter. He stopped, shocked at the difference.

Until now, the apartments were obviously well kept, their inhabitants not rich, but well off enough to afford enough food and clothes. Not so with the scene now before him.

The streets had garbage collecting in the gutters, over-flowing trash bins down one alley stank of something rotten. Graffiti and decades of dirt clung to the outsides of the buildings. The people eyed him with suspicion and thinly veiled hate as he made his way down the block to Starr Flag Avenue.

When he arrived at the spot where the building should have been, Marco's mind reeled.

Half of the structure had been torched, and was caved in, exposing the other half of the building, which looked like it shouldn't have been standing at all. Marco could see scraps of fabric and trash strewn in the barely covered rooms of the burned down apartment building. He checked the address on the slip of paper, and then looked at the addresses on either side.

"This is it," he said to himself, disappointment settling in.

He didn't know what he had expected, but it certainly wasn't a dead end like this.

Stepping over the burned planks and bricks at the front of the building, Marco walked through the exposed side and into the still-standing part. Careful to step where it looked solid, he made his way toward the back.

Though he searched through some of the rubble and looked into every dark corner, Marco didn't see anything but proof of squatters and some very upset rats. He was about to give up when he spotted a staircase leading down into a basement.

Marco stumbled back as a memory burst in his mind:

two boys running down the stairs, their pockets stuffed with sweets, desperate to gorge themselves on their ill-gotten gains.

Taking a few deep breaths to steady the erratic pounding of his heart, Marco stepped down the stairs, careful to avoid those that were badly charred. When he reached the bottom, it should have been dark and gloomy. Instead, there was a faint light coming from a doorway just ahead. He stepped close, trying not to make a sound and peered inside.

The basement apartment had fared better than those upstairs, and it was obviously a favored spot of some of the many homeless of the city. A small kerosene lamp sat to one side and a large battery-operated flashlight was propped up with some old pieces of wood. The floor was covered in a thick layer of dirt. A mattress with a few blankets sat in a corner, along with a duffel bag. Old torn couches sat around the small, square living room, planks of wood supported by cinder blocks and other odds and ends made up a table in the middle, where someone had laid out a bottle of something that could have been wine and a bag of groceries.

"You can come in, I won't bite," said a voice.

Marco gasped at the familiar sound and stepped into the room. Sitting on a dirty leather chair, with stuffing coming out of the arms, was Henry.

"What…what are you doing here?" Marco asked.

Henry sighed, a disappointed sound.

"She didn't do it. You know, the old saying is true, good help really is hard to find."

Marco frowned and stared at the man who'd lived three floors down from him for the past two months.

"Still," Henry continued. "You made it this far, and by the look on your face I'm thinking she jogged something in your memory."

It took him a moment, and then Marco realized what Henry meant.

"The dreams," he said. "Delilah she...that's her power isn't it?"

"Now you're getting it."

Marco took another step further into the room, needing to inspect Henry's face a little more.

He stared up at Marco with eyes that appeared more sunken than ever. A small shiver ran through his painfully thin body and he coughed. The dark stain of a scar circled around his short neck and Marco remembered Delilah's words from a few days ago.

"The ones considered especially dangerous or uncontrollable were given special collars"...Oh crap!

In the dim light, he could see the faintest hint of red in the short dark strands that stuck up on Henry's head.

"If you're trying to find the little boy I was, he's not here," Henry said, a grim set to his wide mouth. "Not really."

"You're Liam."

"In the flesh, such as it is."

The dull ache that had been plaguing Marco since his trip to the library began to burn.

Memories of a summer filled with grief, yet also friendship, exploded in his mind. It was like someone was showing him a movie, but the film had been sped up and the images came at him with such alarming speed that he was having trouble keeping up. As he strained to take it all in, the pain built to an agonizing crescendo until he doubled over from the pain, gulping air into his tight lungs.

"Let it come," Liam said, kneeling down in front of Marco. "The memories taken from you are still there in some way, let them come to the surface, my friend. Remember me."

And Marco did.

Endless summer afternoons running through the streets, stealing sweets from the shops, playing marbles, reading books. Tears when they spoke of family that had been taken from them, Liam's little brother and Marco's mother. Their guilt and fear that it was their fault this had happened, somehow lessening, as they shared it between them. Then that terrible day that Marco had dreamed about, the day Allegra and Dante took his friend from him.

"They took my memories," Marco said, tears running down his cheeks.

"Dante did," Liam said. "It's what he does. And I knew that he'd buried me too deep to simply tell you who I was. I needed someone to find those memories. She helped me escape Lumis, and then she helped me find Delilah, helped me know how to get her out of Lumis."

"She? Liam, I don't understand."

Liam nodded. "I know, I know. It's a lot. Your memories coming back, me being here. But it will all be fine, I promise. The more you remember, and the more I explain. If I can, I don't...It's hard sometimes...to understand how...?"

Liam frowned, looking away as if he were trying to remember something.

"Understand what? Liam, who is 'she'?" Marco asked.

"Sometimes I know, and sometimes it's like a dream. You know how that is, don't you? In any case," he continued. "She called to me, this beautiful voice. I heard it...like the memory of a dream just before you wake up...and it's all so clear and strong...A voice when I was in my cell. She spoke so often to me, showed me how to escape, showed me what I needed to do to help others. I'm just the beginning..."

Marco stared at him as Liam's insanity flowed over his senses, sharp and strong.

"The beginning of what?" Marco asked, though he wasn't sure he wanted to know the answer.

"A new world. One where we can live without fear of being caged like an animal. She told me I could be the one to start it. She promised we would pay them back, pain for pain, and then we'd never have to be afraid again! But first, I wanted to find you."

Liam gave Marco a fevered smile, and it chilled him to the bone.

"You promised, remember?" Liam said. "We promised each other that we'd keep each other safe, that we'd go away, where no one could find us. Well, now we don't have to! Once the rest of us get out and those monsters who caged us are gone for good, there will be nothing to be afraid of!"

Marco stepped back from Liam, hoping even a little distance might help him not be so affected by the man's emotions and that he could get a handle on everything careening through his mind. New memories unfolded every minute, along with new feelings. It made it nearly impossible to keep up with Liam's insane ramblings. On top of all that, his shadows were burning to be let out, but after what he did to Mr. Banks, Marco didn't trust himself.

Especially since I have no idea what Liam's powers are and I'd rather not provoke him.

"I know it's a lot to take in," Liam said. "But I've waited so long to see you again. All those years, I remembered you, my best friend, my only friend. And then she spoke to me, and I knew, you and I, we could be unstoppable! Just like we talked about! And we could lead the others. We could train them to be strong, like us. And no one, anywhere, will ever touch us again. We will be the ones to wound and maim, not them."

"Wound...No, Liam we can't...I'm sure that's not what we wanted."

"No, but it is what we can do now. It's what they've left us with, isn't it?" Liam's voice became hard as he paced the small space in long erratic strides. "They think that they are the power behind us, their puppets, their weapons. But they aren't! We are the power, the weapon! And we control ourselves, don't we? We should be in power, not them, with their small lives and smaller abilities. We are the future, we are the best of them. No one owns us...no one. Never again."

He said that he and I would be unstoppable...and he wore a collar...what are his powers?

Marco met Liam's smiling gaze and decided that he was too tired and overwhelmed for subtlety.

"What are your powers, Liam?" Marco asked.

Liam grinned.

"Let me show you," he said, turning to the doorway. "Come in, Allegra."

Marco turned to see Allegra walk to the doorway, her steps jerky and forced, her hand in the pocket of her coat.

"Take your hand out of your pocket, leave the gun, Allegra."

She did exactly what Liam told her to.

A chill went down Marco's spine and he knew in that moment what Liam's powers were, that he'd made Dr. Brennan kill himself. That he'd orchestrated all this, just to get Marco and Allegra here, for this moment of truth.

"I was hoping you'd be here," Liam said to Allegra, his smile wide and garish in his pale face. "Back where it all started, where you betrayed us."

"Marco," Allegra said, fear reflected in her dark eyes, "you need to leave."

"No! We are just getting started," Liam turned to Marco. "Ask her what you want to know."

He wasn't sure if it was Liam's powers or if he just had to know, but Marco asked, "What happened that day? Where did you take Liam?"

"Tell him, Allegra," Liam said, his words heavy with command.

Allegra's eyes became wide with shock as her mouth opened to speak.

"I took him to a man at a doctor's office."

"And tell him what happened after that."

"He went to a lab, to become an experiment."

Marco stared at her. "Lumis?"

Allegra's jaw clenched.

"Answer whatever questions Marco asks of you, Allegra."

Her eyes became bright with tears and when she spoke it was like someone was pulling the words out of her.

"We didn't know the name of it, and I don't think it was called that then, but yes, essentially."

"Why? Why would you do that, why would you make me forget it?"

"I had just started working at the orphanage, and I was finding powered children, giving them over to a place that was supposed to help them with their powers, give them a normal life. Men from the facility came to me. They wanted me to turn you over to them. I told them you weren't an orphan, that you were like a son to me. They said they could make you an orphan if I didn't cooperate. I realized then that what I'd believed was a lie, that I hadn't been helping those children at all. And I also knew that these men wouldn't stop until they got what they wanted. So, I struck a deal with them, I told them I would find them someone else, equally valuable if they'd leave you alone. I knew about Liam, and I knew no one would miss him, except you. I tried to find someone else, but no one was equal to you. Only Liam."

Marco's stomach twisted, and he ran his hand over his face, seeking the feel of reality.

"My god, Allegra, how could you do something like that?"

"I had no choice. I swore to your mother on the holy rosary to protect you."

"There's always a choice! You could've done something, anything else! What about those people who helped powered people escape? You could've gone to them."

Allegra shook her head. "I formed that group after what happened that summer, there was nothing in place before then! And when they found out what I'd done, the children I'd turned over, they expelled me."

"Can you blame them?" Liam asked, his thin body tense. "Tell the truth."

A sob shuddered past her lips before she spoke.

"No."

"So, you took my memories after that," Marco said.

"Your father and I agreed that you couldn't be burdened with Liam your whole life, especially since you swore you'd find him. We both knew what would happen if you went looking. So, we asked Dante to erase your memories."

Marco felt like someone had punched him in the stomach. "My father knew about this? He asked you to do this?"

"He begged me," Allegra said, tears running down her cheeks. "He'd just lost your mother, he couldn't lose you, too. You had become inconsolable after Liam was taken, angry and combative, using your powers with no regard for who saw you. We had to do something."

"You could've not given them my friend! You could've done anything but what you did!"

"There was nothing else, please, you have to believe me!"

"That's enough, Allegra, be quiet now," Liam said.

Her mouth closed, tears dripping off her chin.

Marco felt his body shake. The shadows under his skin were going wild in their need to be let out. He could taste

Allegra's remorse and fear, Liam's fury and pain. And then his own emotions, spinning in the center of it all like massive, dark storm clouds.

"I can't…" He turned away, his vision going gray, and then back to normal again and again. Liam gasped behind him, and Marco knew that the shadows must be seeping out of his body.

"The day they took me," Liam said, the excitement barely restrained in his voice, "you let those out and engulfed her. I can still remember those screams."

The memory to Marco's mind like a dozen pin pricks. He clutched his head again, and tried to calm himself.

"Do you know what they did to me the first day?' Liam asked, his lips close to Marco's ear, his breath hot and bitter. "They strapped me down and injected me with a solution. It burned as it made its way through my body and I screamed. I screamed for so long that I lost my voice. But, they didn't stop. Not until the first treatment was done."

Marco closed his eyes, trying to shut out the pain Liam was feeling.

"After a week of this, they took me to a room with another child in it. This child had a doll, and she obviously loved it. They told me to make her tear it apart. I wouldn't at first. But after a few hours of electric batons on my back, I did it. The child sobbed, broken hearted."

The emotions were starting to feel like a virus. As it grew stronger, his control over his power weakened.

"Stop," Marco said.

"I thought that was the worst, but no, it was just the beginning. I was their punisher you see, I could make anyone do anything. Blind themselves, burn themselves, throw themselves off a building…though I'd done that before I was imprisoned, so…every time I resisted, desperate to hold onto my humanity, they'd find a way to make me a monster."

Liam's anger began to grow, the revenge he hungered for was a smoldering fire that burned so hot Marco felt singed by it. Somehow, Liam was eroding the weak walls Marco had built up to control himself, and the tide of power within him was rising. If it took over what would he do?

"Stop…please," Marco breathed.

"Over and over again," Liam continued. "They tested me, they made me do things. Until I couldn't feel anything anymore! Except hate for the one who did this to me, to you. She let Dante take your memories, take me!"

The world turned gray and silver, the shadows spilled from Marco's body in a rolling mass. He turned to look at Allegra, who stood frozen in the door way as the shadows crawled up over her.

"You tried that day," Liam said, "but you were just a child, like me. You're not a child anymore, let loose what you want to do!"

Marco grit his teeth as he held back the shadows from digging into Allegra's mind, not knowing if he wanted to spare her or make her hurt as he and Liam had.

The sound of footsteps running down to the basement reached Marco and he hoped they were friendly.

"You brought backup, Allegra?" Liam asked.

The sharp report of a gun going off echoed through the room, and Allegra sprawled forward onto the filthy floor.

With one violent act, the spell Liam had weaved was broken.

Marco ran to Allegra, blood spreading on her shoulder. He turned her over gently, his shadows still writhing around them.

"Marco," she said. "I'm so sorry."

"I know," Marco said, helping her sit up.

She sat against the moldy couch and winced.

"We have to get out of here, before—"

"Mr. Banks says hello," said a man in the doorway.

Marco looked up and saw a short, barrel-chested man with a gun, four others behind him. He was staring at the shadows covering the floor around Allegra and Marco.

How the hell did they find me so fast?

"He said you were a weird one," the man said. "He also said you were supposed to hurt, bad. Let's get this over with, I have a birthday party to get to."

"I think you're going to be late," Liam said.

"That right?"

The man raised the gun to fire at Liam.

"Point the gun to your head," Liam said, his dark eyes feverish.

The man did as he was told, panic starting to light up his eyes. "What...What are you doing, you freak?"

Marco saw the subtle shift in Liam's face too late to stop him.

"Fire the gun."

Blood, bone and brains splattered on the men behind him and the gunman fell to the floor. Marco could taste their terror, heady, as it mixed with Allegra and Liam's emotions.

"Liam," Marco stared at the body. "Stop, you..."

"This is what is necessary, old friend," he answered, turning to the other men. "You—"

"No," Marco said, standing up and directing his shadows at Liam.

They crawled up him as he turned around, jaw slack in disbelief.

"You can't do this," Marco said, not digging into Liam's mind yet, and hoping he wouldn't have to.

"You want to save them? They're here to kill you."

"Maybe. But I don't kill people if I can help it."

Liam stepped toward Marco.

"What have they done to you out here? You and I, we

were meant to be gods! Look at us! What we can do! And you're saving the garbage of humanity?"

"I'm not their judge or god, just a man."

"No, you are so much more," Liam closed the last few feet between them and looked into Marco's eyes. "Find their nightmares and show them."

It was like someone numbed his will and attached puppet strings to him. The shadows flowed in a dark wave toward the remaining gunmen, who tried to run for the stairs. One man managed to make it far enough up the stairs that Marco couldn't reach him with his powers.

The shadows, which had always felt like separate beings from Marco, now truly had a mind of their own. They invaded the minds of the three men, exposing every terror, sorrow and regret. Marco fell to his knees. It was hard to breathe, to think. He was drowning in a sea of emotions that threatened to drive him to the edges of sanity.

"There," Liam said from somewhere. "You see their decay and rot. Do they deserve grace? Does anyone who preys on the weak?"

Marco tried to speak but nothing came out. He could see what Liam spoke of, those impulses, desires and memories were the only things in color in his world right now. They were as bright and garish as the blood and flesh that had been spilled only moments before.

"What does it make you want to do? Do it."

The instinct he'd just barely held back earlier, at Banks' mansion, sprang free of its cage. The shadows pulled on the horrors in the men's minds, amplifying them until it was the only thing the three men were able to see or feel.

"Yes, yes! You are so powerful, it's...it's beautiful!" Liam said, clapping his hands.

Somewhere in the back of Marco's mind, he could feel Liam's control lessen and strained toward that spot. His body shook, sweat drenching him, as he forced himself, inches at a time, toward that precious glimmer of freedom.

The shadows sensed it and violently resisted.

No! I won't give in to this! I won't!

Something screeched in his mind, unnatural and strange and Marco knew that it was the influence of Liam's power. His mind felt like someone was pulling it in two directions at once, but Marco kept going.

The shadows snarled and pulled against him. Marco grit his teeth as he yanked them back, little by little.

I am your master and I say no! Come back!

He pulled again, this time with all the strength he had. In that instant, something snapped in his mind, sharp and blinding.

The shadows rushed back to him and Marco collapsed to the dirty floor, panting.

Liam turned to him, eyes wide. It took Marco a moment to recognize the look as fear.

"No one...you shouldn't have been able to..." Liam said.

"I'm no one's puppet," Marco said, standing up on shaking legs.

The three men lay on the hallway floor. Two were sobbing and one stared into nothing. Marco forced himself to look at them, knowing that even if they could walk out of here, they'd never be whole again, not really. He hadn't been able to stop himself in time and that was something he'd carry the rest of his life.

"You choose these men over your own kind, over me?" Liam asked.

"I choose to—"

"Be a hero?"

Marco was never comfortable with that word. Heroes were bright and hopeful, like Lionel. Hell, even Alice with her dark suit was a beacon of something right and good.

He controlled the dark, the nightmares that tormented good and bad people alike.

"You're too dark for that," Liam said, as if reading his mind. "You and I, we always understood each other."

Marco could feel the truth of what he said, even if he couldn't find the memories that went with it. Lionel and Alice could never shed the last remnant of fear they carried for his powers. And he never blamed them for that, even as it left him feeling lonely at times.

Here, in this broken, shell of a man, was someone who understood the darkness that lived inside of him, and celebrated it.

He'd spent so many years afraid of this power, hating it, trying to understand what it meant that he carried it, what it made him. The moments when he would help someone, save their life, stop a villain, he thought it meant he was good, that darkness obeyed his light. But then, there were the moments when darkness felt so right, so good – when the decision to hold back and deny his darkness seemed like a betrayal.

And I fight against it, as I did today, as I do every day. I have to believe that there's good just in the fight, because if I don't...

He looked at Liam, and though he had compassion for the hell that forged his friend into this vengeful person, he also knew that some of it was also a choice.

"I'm not like you," Marco said, feeling the pain of his words as Liam heard them. "Not anymore."

Liam took a deep breath, his eyes becoming hard and cold, He opened his mouth the speak, but then the sudden stamp of feet above them cut off whatever he was going to say.

"Damn it," Marco said, realizing that the man who had gotten away must have called in others.

Marco went to Allegra and knelt down. "Stay here, alright?"

"Marco," she said, her face pale. "You need to know I-"

"We don't have time for this," Liam said.

"Just stay here," Marco said, as the voices above became louder.

Liam bent down to pick up a gun and tossed it to Marco. "You might need this," he said, grabbing one for himself and heading for the stairs. Marco followed him.

At the top of the stairs they looked up into the burned-out building and saw six armed men searching the rubble for them.

"Can you control them from here?" Marco asked.

"Yes," Liam said.

"No killing."

Liam snorted.

"How many can you control at one time?"

"Two, maybe three, depending on how close I can get," Liam said.

"Clear the way for me."

Marco let his shadows out, and the world turned silver-gray around him. He sought out the two nearest to him and the shadows rolled up their bodies at such speed they barely had time to react. The men behind them gasped, firing their weapons at the shadows, not realizing that they weren't solid. Bullets ripped through the men Marco were manipulating and he felt their deaths barrel through his mind like a truck through a wall. He collapsed onto his knees, gasping for breath.

It was then Marco realized that Liam wasn't beside him. He looked up and spotted Liam running from one of the men and toward another. In a second, the amn Liam had spoken to shot his friend in the leg.

Getting himself past the gut churning sensation of death still lingering on his sense, Marco bolted from the top of the stairway and released his shadows once again, this time at the men who had fired at the shadows. It took seconds for him to find what he wanted and pull on it. He was about to amplify it just a little when a fist collided with his face, sending him sprawling into a pile of burned wood planks.

"You monster!" the man shouted.

It was the one man who had escaped earlier, his eyes wild, spittle flying from his mouth.

Marco scrambled to his feet and barely managed to dodge a punch. The wood underfoot made it incredibly hard to maneuver and he tripped, falling hard on his right arm.

The man pulled Marco up by the front of his duster and punched him hard. Pain shot into his eyes. The man punched again, and Marco tasted blood. In desperation to be released, the vigilante landed a blind kick to the man's knee. He screamed and let Marco go.

He was about to punch the assailant when bullets splintered the rotted wood around him and the man crumpled to the debris strewn floor. Marco dove to the right as more bullets sprayed the air above him.

Damn it, Liam, what are you doing?

He guessed that the the man was probably reloading and peeked up to try and find where he was hiding. If he could find him—

A single gunshot sounded through the din and a man fell from behind a pile of bricks a moment later.

Marco looked up towards the door way that lead to the stairs and saw Allegra leaning against the wall, a smoking gun in her hand.

Allegra swept her arm up and over, firing again. It gave Marco the cover he needed to stand up and find one of the last few assailants, a man with a large rifle. His shadows cascaded toward the man, who had begun firing at Allegra and was too busy to notice the shadows until it was too late. Within moments, Marco had the man running and screaming from imaginary nightmares, his rifle abandoned on the ground.

Marco looked around for Liam, but couldn't find him anywhere.

Of the six men who'd attacked, only two were left standing. One held a rifle, the other a hand gun. They raised them up, and Marco realized that he'd stepped out into the open, no cover anywhere in site.

He released his shadows just as the men pivoted toward the doorway where Allegra still stood.

"No!" Marco screamed, realizing what they were about to do.

The shadows cocooned both men, and Marco pulled quickly on the first thing he could find in their minds. One fell to the ground in shock, the other screamed, his finger pressing down on the trigger in his panic, releasing a steady stream of bullets.

Marco didn't even bother calling the shadows back as he ran toward Allegra, who was sprawled in the doorway. Blood splattered her face from the two bullet wounds in her chest, and sightless eyes stared up at the ceiling.

"No," he moaned, tears falling down his face.

"Too bad," said a voice behind him. "She deserved to suffer more."

Fury, sudden and swift eclipsed his grief and Marco sprang to his feet. Turning and releasing his shadows in one quick motion, he faced Liam.

"Go ahead," Liam said. "Take a peek, see it all. Then tell me I'm wrong."

Marco shook from the grief and rage spilling out of him. He wanted to make Liam feel all of that, to cry and scream in agony.

"Do it. C'mon! Do it!"

There was a tug, small and weak on Marco's will, and

he ignored it. If he was going to torture Liam, it would be by his own choice.

And by god, did he want to in that moment.

But, I'm not like him. And he's been tortured enough.

After a few more seconds, Marco recalled his shadows. Liam slumped forward, breathtaking hate shining from his eyes. Liam turned to the man nearest him that was still conscious.

"Stand up and pick up a gun," he commanded.

The man did.

"Point it at your head, count to twenty, and if Marco tries to come after me before you get to twenty, pull the trigger."

"Damn it, Liam!" Marco said as the man obeyed.

"Sorry, old friend. I've got others to save, and villains to kill."

With that, Liam ran off, sirens whining in the distance, getting closer by the minute.

CHAPTER FIFTEEN

Colleen was tired of waiting for Marco. Cooped up inside the apartment with a hung over man, and a woman, who was wanted by more than one dangerous group of men, made Colleen nervous.

It might have been easier if she could trust Tina, but she had no idea what her mother was going to do. Colleen suspected she'd regret ever bringing the woman into all this. Though Tina had made it clear she didn't want to use Colleen's powers as a weapon within the family business, Colleen didn't know if her mother would make that same decision when it came to a stranger. If her mother could have powered men and women at her beck and call...It was almost as frightening a prospect as Grandfather.

I don't have much of a choice though. I have to trust her...I just hope she's worthy of it.

Sketching usually brought Colleen a measure of peace, a way to retreat from the world. So, she tried it now, getting a pencil and small sketch pad from her bag. However, every face she drew became Karen, the one person she didn't want to think about, and she eventually stashed the pencil and pad back in her bag.

Stepping into the bathroom to splash some cold water on her face, Colleen spotted the deep bathtub and had an idea. When she was younger and wanted to practice her powers without burning down the block, she had thrown fire into the huge claw-foot bathtub in her house. This one wasn't nearly as large, but it would do just fine. She grinned as she took the shower curtain down, surprised at the anticipation she felt.

There was no telling what was coming, what obstacles they would encounter in the next few days, or weeks. Her powers, though frightening to her at times, were a formidable weapon.

If I can get better control, call the flames back...

She flung a small ball of fire into the tub, where it sizzled on the damp surface. Then, concentrating on the ball, Colleen tried to will it back to her outstretched hand. It didn't budge. After a few more tries, Colleen simply scooped it up.

Again and again she tried. Sometimes it looked like the flames reached up toward her hand, and other times they just sat there.

She grunted in frustration just before a soft knock sounded on the door.

"Are you alright?" Delilah asked.

"I'm fine," Colleen said. "You can come in."

Delilah peeked her head around the door, frowning.

"What are you doing?"

"Trying to practice," Colleen said, nodding at a small dancing fireball in the tub. "And I'm terrible at it."

Delilah closed the door and sat on the toilet, her knees brushing against Colleen's back.

"It's called practice for a reason," Delilah said. "What are you thinking about when you try to call it back?"

"I don't know...just...calling it back."

Delilah bit her bottom lip, brows furrowed in thought.

"Did you ever play with a yo-yo?" she asked.

Colleen chuckled. "Well…yeah, why?"

"I loved playing with a yo-yo when I was a kid. I had a bright red one, it was…well, one of the only possessions I had at the time. And I got very good at making it come back to my hand. First, though, I had to get the tug on the string just right."

"Okay, so…?"

"Think of it like a yo-yo. Find just a string of fire on the flame, and tug on it."

Colleen sighed.

I don't have a better idea, might as well try it.

She flung a fireball into the tub, and reached out with her power to divide the flames in front of her.

"Try closing your eyes," Delilah whispered.

"You want me to close my eyes with a fireball in front of me?"

"Trust me."

Colleen sighed again and closed her eyes.

It was hard at first to find the strands of fire within the ball. After a few minutes, Colleen was able to sense the individual flames, the way they danced, their shape and size. She latched onto a rather large one and imagined it like a string attached to her hand.

Behind her Delilah gasped.

Colleen opened her eyes to see a line of flame from the ball to her outstretched hand. She laughed.

"Ok, now tug, just a little," Delilah said.

She did and the ball flew into her hand at such speed that she almost didn't catch it in time.

"You did it!"

Colleen stared at the ball before extinguishing it.

"I don't believe it!" Colleen said, hugging Delilah.

"That was extraordinary. You picked it up so quickly!"

Colleen let her go and stood up.

"Thanks to you."

"No, that was you. Your power is...it's beautiful."

"It's dangerous."

"Isn't everyone's, in some way? I can't burn a house down, but I can make someone remember their worst moments, I can leach information from their minds with a touch."

Colleen stared at her.

"You...You can?"

"And before you ask, no, I haven't done it to you."

If growing up the way she had taught her anything, it was that people were capable of the worst, no matter who they were. Before she could stop herself, Colleen raised a wall of self defense in her mind, trying to protect herself, just in case.

As if she what Colleen was doing, Delilah's dimpled smile disappeared and her lips set into a hard line.

"I didn't—" Colleen began

Delilah turned to leave. "I understand why you don't believe me, and I don't blame you."

"No, wait." Colleen grabbed Delilah's arm. "I'm sorry. I know what it's like for someone to assume they know you, because of one thing, and it's...it's not fair."

"No, but...well, if you've earned distrust...."

Colleen took a deep breath, deciding that it was time to take a plunge into waters she hadn't traversed in some time.

"I trust you," Colleen said.

A laugh that sounded a little bit like a sob flew from Delilah's lips.

"You really shouldn't."

"Everyone has a past. Some of us more than others. Doesn't mean we don't deserve something we can count on, a second chance."

"Is that for you or me?"

Colleen smiled. "Both of us?"

Delilah bit her lip and nodded. "Yeah, I think that would be nice."

"Hey!" Dr. Trace said from the living room. "You two, where are you?"

The sound of a car screeching to a stop, followed by the unmistakable sound of gunfire shattering the windows of the boxing gym downstairs pierced the air.

People on the street began to scream in terror as Colleen and Delilah rushed from the bathroom to find Dr. Trace cowering in fear by the couch.

They ran to the window and saw four cars parked on the street, men with guns standing in front of them. People ran screaming into shops or their cars.

"Damn it!" Colleen said, recognizing one of the men.

Rick was standing with a cigarette in his mouth, gun at the ready, as he motioned for the others to spread out around the boxing gym.

She betrayed me! Damn it, why did I think I could trust her!

"You know them?" Delilah asked from behind Colleen.

"Yes, unfortunately."

"Colleen!" Rick said, taking a long drag from his cigarette and tossing it down. "You know what we want!"

"What do they want?" Delilah asked, her voice full of fear.

Colleen looked over at Dr. Trace and his bloodshot eyes became wide with panic.

"You sold me out!" he said.

"No, but someone found out about you."

"Who?"

Colleen took a deep breath. "Doesn't matter, what does is getting you out of here."

Dante burst into the apartment, dragging a bloodied young man with him. Three others, some with cuts on their sweaty faces, others with a dazed look in their eyes followed him inside the apartment.

"That might be difficult," Dante said, helping the young man onto the couch. "You alright there, Charley?" Charley nodded, clutching a hand on his shoulder, a bloody towel pressed to what Colleen assumed was a bullet wound.

"They surrounded the place," Dante continued. "And there's nothing stopping them from coming in through the gym and straight up here."

"So, why haven't they yet?" Delilah asked.

"Because it's a test," Colleen said, heat building in her body along with a sick sensation in her gut.

Dante's small eyes narrowed."Look Miss Knight, I don't know what you've gotten us all into here, but you find a way to fix it, and fast."

The telephone rang and Colleen knew who it would be.

"How could you?" Colleen asked.

"This is for the best. You have to trust me," Tina said, her voice becoming soft, like she didn't want someone hearing her. "I'm doing what needs to be done."

The heat in Colleen's blood was building fast.

"No," she breathed. "You can't...you'll kill Karen...no."

"Now isn't the time for dramatics or to worry about casualties. There are bigger concerns here."

A roar started in her ears, like the sound of the ocean.

"No," Colleen whispered.

"Get a hold of yourself and just give the man over!"

"No!"

Power flooded through Colleen's body, like a swollen river of molten heat that had been damned up far too long. Her vision became bright, orange and white all at once, and she could smell smoke from the melting receiver in her hand. It dropped in two halves to the floor and Colleen turned around.

Dr. Trace scrambled back from her while Delilah stared

at her, mouth open. Dante swore, crossing himself and the boxers did the same.

Without a word, Colleen walked out of the apartment and down the stairs. She wasn't aware that her body glowed with power or that her eyes had become twin flames. The power she'd feared and loved all her life was a living thing inside of her. If she stopped and thought about it, Colleen would be hard pressed to know why now, after all these years, the power was both raging and yielding.

The calm she felt in the midst of her fury was like being bathed in sunlight. She could see herself and what she was about to do, instinct taking over, as she kicked the back door open where men were waiting to shoot her. They were good shots, quick and guiltless when it came to their jobs. Colleen was faster, bolts of flames shooting from her hands at such speed that the men had no time to run before they were set aflame.

Someone came around the corner of the gym to her left. Bullets barely missed her as bits of siding splintered and spewed behind her. Another bolt shot from her hands, hitting the man with such force that he flew back into the alley, writhing on the ground as flames consumed him.

Two more ran down the alley and met the same fate as Colleen bolted toward where Rick and his cronies were stationed out front. She knew that she was killing them, knew that what she was doing was wrong, but that fact was distant in her mind, something she would face later.

Gunfire erupted ahead of her, but none of it was coming down the alley. She looked around the corner, her vision still too bright, like an over exposed picture. Rick and the others had taken cover behind their cars, and bullets rained down on them from above.

Colleen smiled. *Delilah, you gutsy beauty.*

While they were busy defending themselves against Delilah, and the others, Colleen shot fire at the ones most exposed. The screams of the men as they burned, the smell of their charred flesh, reached Colleens senses at last and gave her pause, just for a moment. Then, through the chaos in front of her, she saw Rick turn and meet her stare. His full lips quirked into a grin and he fired at her through the smoke and flames. The bullets struck the gym, spraying paint and splinters in her face. Her eyes stung and she bent over, wiping at them.

When she looked up, Rick had managed to get the few remaining men to charge into the boxing gym. Colleen ran around the corner and was forced back by more gunfire. She turned and ran back down the alley, planning on going through the back door, when she was startled by bullets pinging around her, hitting garbage bins and the side of the building.

A man on each end of the alley held rifles and started advancing on her. Colleen could still feel the soft roar of power infusing her body with heat, though it was waning, and a distant feeling of fatigue was starting to build. When she really looked at the men advancing on her, she could tell they were afraid of her.

I can use that.

"Back off," she said, "and I won't roast you alive."

They actually stopped in their tracks for a second, but then one decided he could get the jump on her and fired. The bullets grazed her shoulder and thigh, the burning sting of the wounds making her power roar in her ears in defense.

She unleashed it. The men ran from the inferno, one of them not fast enough to escape it as the fire licked up his legs and back. He rolled around on the damp, cold ground to stamp it out. Through sheer force of will, Colleen ignored the bodies lying in front of the back door, and ran inside, gunfire echoing down from the apartment.

If they hurt Delilah I'll —

A fist careened out of the shadows and connected with her jaw. The force sent her into a stack of boxes. Another fist connected with her stomach. She looked up into Rick's face and another punch landed across her cheek. It sent her to the floor in front of the now toppled stack of boxes.

Screams sounded from above, followed by what sounded like someone or something falling to the ground. Then feet running, someone begging for help.

"You need to believe me when I say," Rick said, "this is for the best."

"Go to hell," she said.

She was about unleash a bolt of flame at him, taking her chances on burning the place to the ground, when Rick kicked her in the stomach. Air was suddenly very hard to come by and she coughed.

Footsteps ran past her, followed by the sound of something being dragged. Colleen looked up and saw Dr. Trace being carried between two men.

Grandfather and Tina can't get him…but maybe if I just make them think I'd kill him.

She knew the risk and that Marco might never forgive her if something went wrong, but in that moment, the larger picture loomed before her and there was only one thing to do.

The power that had propelled her only minutes before was ebbing fast, probably because of the air that was still hard to get into her lungs, but she had enough to create a ball of flame and fling it at Dr. Trace.

"No!" Rick screamed.

Too late.

The men dragging the doctor turned, dropped the unconscious man between them and flung themselves out of the way. Colleen watched as the fireball landed on Dr. Trace, then, with the tool that Delilah had taught her just that morning, she grabbed at the individual flames, trying to bring it back before it consumed him.

Rick didn't know that she was actually trying to minimize the damage to Dr. Trace, only that she'd cost him a valuable asset.

He yanked her up by the collar of her shirt just as she was grabbing a thin strand of flame and punched her once, twice, three times in the face.

Colleen lost control and let go of the strand, which somehow made the ball spread out and over Dr. Trace's body. In moments he was enveloped in flames.

"You have no idea what you've done!" he said, punching her one last time.

She saw feet run past her just before the world went black.

CHAPTER SIXTEEN

"C'mon, Colleen, wake up!"

Colleen felt something cold and wet on her face. Cool air was flowing over her body. Her mind felt swathed in cotton, thoughts fuzzy and hard to define. She tried to open her eyes, one of them refusing to do so all the way.

"Oh, thank god!" Delilah said, a wet washcloth in her hand. "What happened?"

Colleen moved and immediately regretted it. Her head throbbed like someone was driving a railroad spike into it. She lay on the concrete floor of the back room for another few minutes, before she felt like she could move without throwing up. Delilah helped her sit up. Colleen held her head in her hands as black spots dotted her vision. Soon, they disappeared, along with the nausea that had come upon her.

When Colleen looked up, she saw Dante talking to someone, the boxers standing around giving her wary glances.

"What's going on?" she asked.

"The police are here," Delilah whispered. "Dante is

talking to one of them now, he says he can minimize things."

Colleen looked to where Dr. Trace's body should be, but only a dark stain remained on the cement floor.

"Where is…?" Colleen couldn't bring herself to say it.

"I think they took the body with them," Delilah said. "The other bodies are still out there, though."

Colleen closed her eyes. The memory of what she'd done, the purity of purpose she'd felt in the moment…it would haunt her the rest of her life.

"Stop," Delilah said, her voice hard. "You have to stop this guilt. It does nothing."

"I killed them, without a second thought."

"And they would've done the same to us."

"That's why it's not right. I have to be different than them!"

Delilah paused. "You are."

Colleen shook her head. "Not enough. And maybe I won't ever be."

"Use it, then. It's a part of you. Stop trying to avoid it and find a way to use it. Because one way or another it's going to come out."

The phone in the office nearby rang several times and Delilah ran toward it. As Delilah spoke in low tones, Colleen realized that after the beating she took, she should feel much worse. She looked at where the bullets had grazed her shoulder and thigh, eyes wide with astonishment. They were tender and bruised, but the wounds had scabbed over. She touched her jaw, where a huge lump should be and, though it was very tender, there was nothing to indicate she was seriously hurt.

Do my powers help me heal faster? I've never fought this way since I discovered them…That's…kind of amazing!

Delilah walked toward her, face tense.

"It's for you," she said.

Colleen winced as she got to her feet, clutching her head and wishing her powers had healed everything while she'd been knocked out.

Guess I should be grateful I'm not bleeding on the cement though.

"Who is it? Marco?"

Delilah shook her head.

"A woman, she—"

Colleen practically ran to the office, ignoring the violent throbbing of her head.

"We need to talk," Tina said, her voice tight. "Now."

"You think I'm going to—"

"Yes. I do."

Colleen paused, fire simmering in her blood.

Maybe Dr. Trace is alive, maybe there's a way to make this work after all. If I can get her on my side, get her to somehow protect Karen and not turn Dr. Trace over to Grandfather.

"All right, where?" she said.

"My office, quick as you can."

It took Colleen a good half hour to get out of the boxing gym, even with Dante and his police connection running interference. People were still huddled in their homes or businesses; the streets having been blocked off by the police, who weren't sure if the powered person who had burnt the gunman to a crisp was still on the loose or not.

Colleen shoved her hands into her coat pockets and refused to look at the bodies that were being loaded into a van from the morgue as she walked out of the gym and down the street. She had borrowed a scarf and sunglasses from Allegra's desk to hide the bruises and cuts on her face, plus her hair, which was ruined by the fight. Her clothes smelled of smoke and something else that she chose to ignore, as she tried to run the two blocks to get a cab. Her wounds might be healing unusually fast, but she was still hurting.

The first two blew right past her. The third one stopped mostly because she'd stepped in front of it.

"You crazy or something!" the cabbie said.

"I need to get to 42nd and Mariah," she said, getting inside before he could drive away.

"You got money?"

Colleen dug the wad of bills from her emergency stash out of her coat pocket and showed him.

"Extra for getting me there as fast as you can, and I mean fast, not tourist speed."

The cabbie smiled, teeth yellow flashing. "Alright, then."

Five minutes in, Colleen seriously contemplated walking, at least she'd get there alive.

The cabbie dodged pedestrians and sped down narrow streets that were no better than glorified alleys. The man's crazed driving caused Colleen to have to grab the handholds to keep from sliding across the back seat. Soon, the cab screeched to a halt outside the elegantly sad Torch and Grier Theater. She paid him extra as promised and the cab sped off.

Colleen stood on the side walk and stared up at the brick and glass front of the theater. It had been the best jazz club on this side of the city back in the day, and a well-respected gin joint before then. The marquis, which used to glow with pride, announcing the latest singer, was dark, as it had been for most of Colleen's life. Even the letters that used to say "Opening Soon" were now mostly gone. The glass doors, with their gold trim, were boarded up, whether from being broken or to protect them.

Colleen walked down the right side of the building to

the stage door, knocking out the secret code. A moment later, the locks clicked and the door groaned open.

To reveal Rick.

Flames leapt to her fingers and she widened her stance, ready for a fight.

"Cool it," he glared at her hand. "Literally."

For a second, she let him wonder if she would, then closed her hands around the flames and walked through the door.

The smell of the theater had never left this place, as if the ghosts of singers and performers still haunted it, their grease paint, sweat and alcohol lingering long after they'd gone. The backstage area was wide and open, without sets or instruments to clog it up. New lights overhead shone with golden light as Rick led her to the back, and to stairs that led to the upstairs offices.

Rick opened the door for her and Colleen stepped through into her mother's office.

"Go back and wait for him," Tina said to Rick.

Rick hesitated, and Colleen was surprised to see fear in his eyes.

"He's coming here?"

Tina leveled a hard look at him and didn't answer. Rick sighed and closed the door behind Colleen. She looked around and was surprised at how little had changed since the last time she was here.

The walls were still a buttery yellow that contrasted beautifully with the richly colored prints on the wall. Colleen recognized one of them as an Archibald Motley and wondered where Tina had gotten such a rare work.

File cabinets lined one wall, and a table with expensive liquor and a coffee maker sat along the opposite wall. Her mother's desk was a beautiful light wood antique that Colleen remembered once sitting in the library of the brownstone she'd grown up in. She had learned to write while sitting in her mother's chair, pretending to be her. On top of its gleaming surface were two trays full of neatly stacked papers and a fancy pen set next to a red cup of pencils, all the same height.

A door on the right led to a small bathroom. The one to the left was a large closet with a trap door that led to a space just large enough for a person or several cases of gin to hide.

Tina stood up and came around her desk, curvy body tight like a coiled spring. Colleen took an instinctive step back, recognizing the look on her face, the energy coming off her mother in waves.

"You mucked up the works this time, that's for certain," she said.

Colleen didn't trust herself to speak, so she just kept silent.

"There was more going on here than you know," Tina said. "I had a plan, and you just couldn't do what you were told, like always."

A swift knock on her door and one of her lackeys peeked his head in.

"His car just pulled up."

Tina swore and waved the man off.

"He's early, just perfect," she looked at Colleen and said, "Get in the closet."

"What? No!"

Tina's dark eyes became hard with both fear and anger

"Get in the damn closet, Colleen. And keep your mouth shut. If you can for once do what you're told, we might all make it out of this mess alive."

Colleen hesitated, then headed for the closet.

Maybe I'll learn what's going on here.

She had just positioned herself behind the coats and extra changes of clothes when the sound of a door opening reached her, followed by with footsteps.

"Mr. Price," Tina said. "How nice to see you again."

"Mrs. Knight," said a man with a voice as smooth as silk. "You have an interesting way of fulfilling our bargain. I'm not sure my employer will be pleased."

"You got what you wanted."

"Yes and no."

There was a pause, the sound of heavy feet pacing the small office.

"And now you don't have to worry about him talking," Tina said.

Colleen could hear the barest hint of worry in her voice and wondered who this was that could elicit that kind of emotion from her mother.

"I suppose that's true," Mr. Price said, a hint of anger under the cordial tone. "Now, for what you wanted out of this."

There was a rustling of some kind, then a thud, as something heavy was placed on what Colleen assumed was Tina's desk.

No one spoke for a moment, then Tina said, "And the other part of our agreement?"

"You should be getting a phone call soon to inform you of the sad passing of your father. The rest is up to you."

"And no one will know that he was poisoned?"

"Not unless they do a rather thorough autopsy. But I'm sure you can convince them that's unnecessary."

"Then, our business is finished."

Mr. Price chuckled, the sound sent chills down Colleen's spine.

"I've heard some interesting reports today," he said.

"Oh?"

"Tell me, Mrs. Knight. Are you speaking with your daughter?"

Colleen's mouth went dry and she could feel the heat

gathering within her. She clamped down on the feeling. This was no time to lose control.

"Not in years, why?" Tina answered.

"No reason. It's just that usually powers run in the family, and since your son had an interesting ability, I just assumed your daughter might as well."

"I only recently learned of my son's abilities. My daughter...well, she was never forthright with me about anything, other than her hatred of me."

Mr. Price laughed again. "Ah yes, children. How they grow to hate their parents. Well, I was only curious."

Tina didn't say anything and Colleen imagined her staring down this man as the silence stretched.

"Is there anything else?" Tina asked, her tone icy.

"I suppose not," Mr. Price said. "Not right now anyway. I'll call on you if there is."

"Within the confines our agreement, of course."

"Of course."

Colleen heard the footsteps again and the door closing. She waited until her mother opened the closet door before stepping out. The first thing she saw was a plain urn sitting on her mother's desk, the kind that held cremation ashes.

Tina picked it up and stared at it.

"This is supposed to be your brother," she said.

Colleen swallowed. "Supposed to be?"

Tina smirked and set it down. "I'd be a fool to believe anything that man said."

"Who was it?"

"He goes by Mr. Price, though I'd wager that isn't his real name. He's a high-level lackey for someone else."

"Who?"

"Probably the real power behind Lumis. He came to me with a deal. Said that he could get me Andrew's remains in exchange for Dr. Trace."

"And killing Grandfather?"

"Oh, that had been in the works for months now. Mr. Price fancies himself a man of many interests, and since Grandfather told him to take a flying leap, he came to me, to see if I'd be more open to a partnership of sorts."

Colleen's eyebrows rose.

"Don't worry," Tina waved her hand. "I'm in control here. He just wants a little extra muscle at his disposal. The kind that can't be traced back to him."

Probably to kidnap more powered children. The sick son of a—

"But this," Tina said, picking up the urn. "Is not your brother."

"How do you know?"

"It's too convenient, for one. And for another, there's no way Mr. Price, and whoever he works for, would let a man with the talents your brother has die."

A disgusted smile graced Colleen's lips. "You knew about his powers all along."

"Of course I did."

"What are they?"

Tina hesitated. "First, I need to know if I can count on you."

"For what?"

"I need to get Andrew back, and I know that either Lumis has him or…"

"Andrew is going to make a move against you."

"Yes. Before he went missing, Grandfather had gotten his hooks in him good. Andrew had always known the score, that I was the one that would take over, since you were gone. He thought that if he could be indispensable to Grandfather, he'd take over."

"Now that you're in control, though, he'll try to take you out."

Tina nodded.

"I won't kill him for you," Colleen said.

"I wasn't asking you to."

"What then?"

"I want him back. I want a chance to correct what Grandfather did, and have us all together again."

Colleen laughed, a bitter sound that made Tina's eyes harden. "I'm not coming back."

"Fine," Tina said. "But at least help me get your brother back."

"And if he doesn't want to come back?"

Tina looked at the urn and shook her head. "He will. Andrew never could stay away from us. He just has to know that he can come back."

Colleen studied Tina, the perfectly hard and confident facade that hid the fear and pain underneath. She'd almost missed it in her anger at Tina for what happened earlier.

I still can't trust her. When it comes down to it, she'll always choose herself. And if Andrew doesn't want to come back, she can't have him out there plotting against her. But if I can be in on it all, I can protect him, get him away from her and this, once and for all.

She knew the gamble she was taking, how easily everything could fall apart, with her caught in the crossfire between Andrew and her mother. Her brother was worth it though.

"Alright," she said, "but only for Andrew. After it's settled, I'm done."

"Are you now? So easy to quit your family. How's that worked for you so far?"

Colleen just stared at her, eyes narrowed, lips pursed.

"Alright," Tina said. "I'll leave you be after this. If that's what you really want. Your brother's powers are the control, creation and manipulation of ice."

Colleen's lips parting in surprise.

"When he disappeared," Tina continued, "he could turn small amounts of water into ice, though he couldn't shape it into anything. But now, with whatever they've done to him in that lab, his powers are stronger, deadlier."

Tina handed Colleen a file. "Your Grandfather was a thorough man. He had dozens of files on Lumis Chemical, don't ask me how he got so much information, but he did."

Colleen opened it, her eyes widening at what she saw.

"Blueprints...the underground labs?" Colleen asked.

Tina nodded. "The fire above did some damage to that lab, and until recently, they've had too much attention on the lab to move everything from the secret facility underneath. They've started moving some things and people this week. But I have it on good authority that they're moving the most dangerous people tonight."

"And you want me to waltz in there and get Andrew out?"

"Well, fighting would be better, but yes, that's the idea."

"How the hell am I supposed to do that?" Colleen asked, looking at the piece of paper with the breakdown of security in the secret lab. "Look at—"

"The staff is decreased," Tina said. "At least in half. Only absolutely necessary personnel."

Colleen's eyes narrowed. "How do you know that?"

"I have my spies."

"More like expendables," Colleen said, not quite under her breath, as the phone rang.

Tina didn't even flinch at the comment and turned to answer her phone.

"What are the charges? I see...alright, do what you have to...yes, it is..."

She dropped the receiver into its cradle, then dug into her desk drawer for a set of car keys.

"Here," she handed them to Colleen. "You will need help. At present, your boss is down at the police station in the Irish Quarter. By the time you get there, he should be out of questioning."

Colleen stared at Tina and shook her head. "Why would you help him?"

"Like I said, you'll need help. Take the file folder. It's got a keycard, and you'll need to memorize the layout. Inside, you'll also find instructions for when to go in, and where Andrew likely is."

"How do you know he's even still there?"

"I don't. But if there's a chance…"

"We have to take it."

Tina nodded.

Colleen looked at the folder and back up at her mother. "A day ago, you didn't want me near this, and now you want me to go and get Andrew. Why the change of heart?"

Tina looked down at her desk, running her fingertips slowly across its polished surface.

"You're the only person I can trust," she finally said.

Colleen's lips parted in shock and she shook her head. "Not even Rick?"

"No, not even Rick."

Mother and daughter looked at each other, and for a moment, the refuse of their past was shoved aside and they could see one another. Colleen felt exposed, but also known. Tears sprang to her eyes.

"Mom…"

"No," Tina said, her voice rough. "Someday, you and I will lay it all out. And, maybe we'll understand each other at the end of it. But that someday is not today. I need you sharp on this, so you…so you come back. You hear me?"

Colleen nodded, forcing the tears back.

"Good," Tina said, waving her hand at Colleen. "Now, go on. The car should be just outside."

Colleen wanted to linger, but she knew her mother was right, this wasn't the time. So, she walked out of the office and down the stairs to the alley outside. Waiting for her was a beautiful black Ford Starliner with blood red leather seats. Colleen let out a snort of laughter and shook her head.

"What, you don't like it?" Rick asked, glaring at her.

"It's a little ostentatious but…" Colleen slid into the driver side and put her hands on the wheel. "Yes, I do."

"Don't do anything stupid."

"Why Rick, I didn't think you cared."

Rick glanced up at where Tina's office would be, and then back to Colleen. "I don't. At least, not about you."

Colleen's grin faltered and she understood. "Take care of her. Some aren't going to like her taking Grandfather's seat at the table."

"I know my job," Rick said. "You just stay out of our way."

"Wish I could," Colleen said, driving away.

CHAPTER SEVENTEEN

Marco recognized some of the officers that had shown up to investigate the gunshots at the burned-out apartment building, and it wasn't a pleasant reunion. They'd cuffed him and thrown him in the back of a squad car without so much as a question. He'd at least gotten to make a phone call, though it took far more rings than it should have for someone to pick up at the boxing gym.

"Hello?" said Dante.

The sound of the man's voice brought an instant rage that took Marco by surprise.

He took my memories...And I have to ask for his help now.

"It's Marco," his teeth were clenched, knuckles white as he clutched the receiver. "I'm at the police station."

"Where's Allegra?"

Marco told Dante what he could. The other end went silent long enough for Marco to wonder if it had gone dead.

"Dante? Are you still there?"

A sharp sob came through and Marco felt like he'd been cut in two. A part of him was almost glad that Dante was hurting after what the man had done to him. And another part, the part that felt Allegra's lose no matter what she'd done, shed tears right along with him.

"I...I can't...Oh god Marco she's gone!"

"Yeah...What's going on there? I need to talk to Colleen."

It took Dante several minutes to calm down long enough to tell Marco everything that had happened.

By time Dante was finished, Marco felt sick.

"Dr. Trace is dead," he whispered.

"Yeah and...it's a mess here kid. Look I'll get one of the boys down there with the bail and—"

"No. Don't bother."

"Marco—"

"I'll figure this out. I don't want *your* help Dante. I don't want anything from you. Ever again."

Marco slammed the receiver down and leaned his head on the cool surface of the wall.

Everything he'd worked for, and sacrificed for, relationships with people he'd once trusted with is very life. It had all gone up in flames today and all Marco could taste was ash.

He couldn't even think of what to do next, his mind was a chaotic landscape of loss and anger. It was only when an officer pulled on his shoulder and brought him back to the interrogation room that Marco could do anything other than stare blank eyed at nothing.

"So," said the smug detective across from him, "let's start with why the hell you were found surrounded by dead bodies."

After an hour or more of questions that Marco answered with little feeling or care, he began to wonder if this time his luck would run out, that they'd find a way to pin something on him.

The faces of the men whose minds he broke, Allegra's vacant stare, even Liam's insane smile were on a constant loop in his mind. He wasn't so sure that he didn't deserve some kind of punishment.

"It's your lucky day, I guess," said the detective who had been interrogating him, as he came back into the room.

"Why's that?" Marco asked, his voice flat.

The detective unlocked the handcuffs and scowled at him. "Two witnesses and someone with deep pockets."

Marco frowned.

"Get out of here," the detective said. "And I'd tell you to keep your nose clean, but I really hope you don't."

Marco hesitated another second before getting to his feet. "What about Allegra?" he asked.

"That's a matter for the coroner. Take it up with them."

Marco swallowed the grief that threatened to choke him and walked out of the room into a sea of desks and blue uniforms. Stale coffee stung his nose and the clacking of typewriters and voices felt louder than it should have, as if his senses were still heightened after the conflict with Liam.

Anger, hate, even a little fear, swirled in a dark tangle through his mind from the men and women around him. Some of it was directed at him, some of it for other people in the building. The shadows had been relatively quiet since being unleashed on the three men earlier. Now, their movement was distant, gentle, like children shifting in their sleep. Marco got the distinct impression that somehow, they had been taught, at last, that they weren't in control.

If it took all this to accomplish that, it wasn't worth it.

He stopped by the front desk, asking the woman for the number of the coroner who had taken Allegra's body. The woman's sigh was laced with aggravation as she shoved a slip of paper at him, with the phone number on it, along with some paperwork to fill out. She didn't even look up when he'd filled it out and handed it back.

For a moment, Marco just stood there, exhaustion and grief making his limbs and mind heavy.

"You need something else?" the woman asked.

"No," Marco said, turning away.

He made it to the glass front doors before realizing he had no money and no way to get back to the boxing gym. He'd have to walk back, and the thought made him wish for a night in a cell, after all.

Maybe if I just sit for a minute.

The metal chairs in the small lobby of the station had a thin cushion on them, which did nothing to make them more comfortable. Marco didn't care, as he sat, elbows on his knees, face in his hands. Minutes slipped past, and still he sat, the events of the past few days running in a loop through his mind. He'd been so close to success and everything had fallen apart. Again.

Delilah...she was working with Liam, she used me...Liam... Allegra...Dante. All those lies, those secrets. And me in the middle of it all, not even knowing...

"Well, don't you look pathetic," said a voice next to him.

Marco looked up to see Colleen standing over him, her face bruised and cut. When he looked into her eyes, however, he could see her sympathy and understanding, as if she'd also lost things today.

"C'mon," she held out her hand, "we've still got work to do."

They were nearly at the door, when a round-faced officer came into the station. He looked like he'd been in a fist fight not too long ago and lost. Colleen stopped midstep and Marco could feel her fear like a cold spike to the heart. He looked at the officer, who glared at Colleen as he passed.

"You okay?" he asked her quietly.

She took a deep breath, looked back at the retreating figure of the officer.

"Yeah...I just...yeah, let's go."

CHAPTER EIGHTEEN

"What happened?" Marco asked as Colleen slid into the driver's side of the car.

He could barely appreciate the soft leather that cradled his tired body. Though he needed to know more details about happened at the boxing gym, a part of him just wanted to close his eyes, lean back into the head rest, and shut the world out.

Colleen pulled away from the curb and into the early evening traffic. She told him, with a voice full of regret, how she'd called her mother to ask for help with Grandfather, and the consequences of it. In halting words, Colleen admitted to losing control, and burning not only the men who were attacking her, but Dr. Trace as well.

"I'm sorry," she said, eyes focused on the tail lights in front of them. "I...I know that doesn't help anything."

Marco sighed. "No, it doesn't. Is Delilah...is she alive, did they take her?"

"She's fine, as much as she can be."

Marco nodded, relieved. In spite of everything, the last thing he wanted was Delilah to get hurt or taken back to Lumis.

"If your mother is telling the truth, if she has all your Grandfather's research, then maybe there's something in all of it we can use," Marco said. "Do you think she'd let us take a look?"

"I don't know. Maybe, if we do what she's asked of us."

"Which is?"

Colleen's gaze slid to him for a moment before handing him the file folder from the glove box.

Marco looked over the information, his gut twisting in both fear and anticipation. Blueprints, keycodes, guard rotations, even the shipping company that was loading "sensitive equipment and specimens". The last page of the file had a slip of paper with curled, precise writing that said: "Look in the trunk."

"Have you?" Marco asked.

"Have I what?" she asked.

He held the note up. "Looked in the trunk?"

She glanced at the note and swore under her breath.

"That's Tina, my mother's, handwriting. And no, I haven't."

"We probably should."

Colleen sighed. "Yeah, probably."

"What's the catch in all this?"

"Tina thinks that my brother is still there. She says that security will be vulnerable and we can get in and get him."

"What then? I mean, is that it? We get your brother and she doesn't ask anything else of me, or you?"

Colleen paused, lips pressed together. "I have no idea," she finally said.

Marco sighed, Liam's last words ringing in his head.

Liam will be going there, he might already be there. I could catch him, stop him from killing anyone else. But what then? What the hell do I do with what they made him?

He ran a hand over his face and closed his eyes.

"What aren't you telling me?" Colleen asked.

"A lot…and…" He turned to her. "Look, I don't need an assistant anymore, I need a partner, and I think you do, too. So, how about it? Can I trust you to watch my back, and I'll watch yours?"

"For tonight or…?"

"How about for as long as we need it?"

Colleen grinned, tears shining in her eyes. "I think I'd like that."

He smiled back. "All right. There's people at Lumis that we both need to get tonight, and mine is…well, dangerous is putting too fine a point on it."

Marco filled her in on what had happened, who Henry really was, what Allegra and Dante had done to him. By the time he was finished, they had arrived at the boxing gym.

Colleen stared ahead, eyes wide.

"You're serious?" she asked after a moment.

"I wish I wasn't."

"I'm so sorry."

"Thanks," he looked out his window and swore. "My god…"

"Yeah."

The front of the gym was riddled with bullets, shards of glass clung to the window frames, with the rest scattered on the polished wood floor inside. Yellow tape stretched like garish ribbons across the front of the gym and the front door hung to the side on one hinge. Marco could see through the broken windows that the equipment inside was largely untouched.

Marco and Colleen walked around to the back, chalk marks outlining several bodies. He looked at Colleen, who stared at one of them, grief tight on her face.

In the back room it wasn't much better. The smell of smoke clung to everything, and scorch marks could be seen on the floor between toppled over boxes.

Dante stood amongst all this, attempting to sweep but

really just pushing glass and dirt around. When he looked up, tears slid down his weathered cheeks.

"Thank god, Marco!" he said, reaching out to embrace Marco, who flinched away, anger and grief boiling inside of him, making the shadows twitch.

"I know what you did," Marco said, his voice low and rough.

Dante's eyes grew large and he took a step back. "Kid, look—"

"There's nothing you have to say about it that I want to hear."

"Marco…"

"Nothing!"

Dante's mouth snapped shut, a hard look replacing the sad one from a moment before.

"Is Delilah still here?" Colleen asked.

Dante nodded. "She's upstairs."

"You need to call whoever it was that was supposed to get her. Tell them she'll be waiting at Allegra's house," Marco said, walking toward the stairs. "And then, I never want to see you again."

Dante didn't say a word, just nodded and went to the office.

Colleen followed Marco up the stairs to the apartment.

"Marco," Colleen said, putting her hand on his arm before he reached the door, "go easy on her. She didn't have much choice."

Marco looked down at the floor, his jaw tightening under his beard, before opening the door. He wanted to believe Colleen. Hell, in a way, he did. It couldn't minimize the stab of betrayal though, and that was what lived in him at the moment.

Delilah sprang up from the couch, golden hair gleaming in the low light of the lamp.

"Marco! Oh my god, I was so scared!" She ran to him and threw her arms around his neck.

Marco's hands clenched at his sides. After a moment, Delilah pulled back to look him in the eyes. The sadness that flowed from her was almost overwhelming.

"You know," she said, stepping away from him.

Her shoulders sagged and she looked so tired and worn, as if she just wanted a place to lay her head and feel safe, and couldn't find one.

"I'm going to go see what my mother left us in the trunk," Colleen said. "You?"

"We'll be fine," Marco said.

Delilah nodded at Colleen.

Once the door closed, Marco and Delilah just stared at the floor. When Marco did look at her, he could see tears running down her cheeks.

"Why?" he asked, cringing at the way he sounded like a broken-hearted child. "Was it all a game? Me and you, was it…"

"No."

"And after everything, I'm just supposed to believe you?"

"You could use your powers," she stepped up to him. "Go ahead. See for yourself."

He didn't have to, he could feel the truth of her words.

"I would've done anything to escape, to have a normal life," she said. "Liam got word to me during my last mission, told me who to trust and what the plan was. He set the fire, and when I escaped, he told me that he could get me to safety. The price was to get you to remember him."

"Sleeping with me, was that just part of it all?"

"No. I need you to understand. I'd established a connection with you a week before we met, but whatever Dante had done, your memories were buried too deep. I had to have physical contact with you to find them. When we kissed, that was all I needed to get deeper access to your mind. I didn't expect to...I never met anyone like you. For the first time in my life I realized that I could have someone of my own choosing and I wanted you. That was real. That didn't have anything to do with Liam."

For the first time...she'd never had a choice before.

He swallowed, his anger cooling a bit as he saw one more picture of what her life had been like.

"Why didn't you tell me?" he asked.

"I didn't want you to look at me like you are now. I hoped Liam might keep his mouth shut if he got what he wanted."

"And then what? You stay and we...?"

Delilah looked away. "Is that so insane?"

Marco opened his mouth to say yes, it was. But he couldn't.

It's not actually. She and I... Though, not anymore.

"I know that what I did wasn't right," she said, looking up at him again. "I'm sorry I hurt you. Truly, Marco."

He could feel the heat of her body, her breath like desperate feathers against his face. She wanted to be held, kissed and forgiven, he could see it, feel it coming off her in waves. A part of him wanted that. To drown this day in the passion of her embrace.

But there was work to be done, and he wouldn't let himself be taken for a fool by her again.

Marco stepped away, pacing a few steps toward the bathroom and back again, needing distance from her.

"What's next?" she asked. "Are you going to turn me in or...?"

"You're staying at Allegra's until tomorrow, when the group picks you up."

She nodded.

"But before then," Marco said, "I need some help."

"With what?"

Marco handed her the file folder. The moment she opened it, her blue eyes bulged and she gasped.

"You're going into Lumis? Are you insane?"

"No, but Liam is, and he's going there to free the powered people and kill the rest."

"No." She shook her head. "That's not possible. There's no way Liam would go back there, no sane person would."

"He's not exactly sane. Kept going on about a 'she' that spoke to him and wanted him to do things. I think he's —what?"

Delilah's already pale skin became paper white, as she stared at him.

"What do you know?" Marco asked.

"He said...he said 'she' spoke to him?"

"Yes, why? Does that mean something to you?"

Delilah swallowed as if she were about to be sick.

"For some of us," she said, her voice barely above a whisper. "Those with mental powers...we hear someone, a voice that's sometimes loud, and other times quiet. Liam...I think because his powers are so strong, he must've heard her more than others."

"Who is it?"

"We don't know, we didn't even talk about it that much, except in hushed whispers. The lab men and women would...they'd try to 'cure' us of hearing the voice, so we stopped talking about it. But...it's a powered person, an exceptionally strong one, that is constantly trying to reach some of us."

"Why?"

"I wish I knew. I never got more than half sentences and barely remembered dreams. Liam, if he's doing what the voice said, he must've had a stronger connection."

Marco ran a hand over his face and sighed.

Another unknown! Damn, this whole case keeps getting bigger and stranger!

"Do you know who it is or where she is?" he asked.

"No, I don't even know if she's real or just something some of us have made up."

"Alright, so she's probably not at Lumis."

"I wouldn't think so, no." Delilah reached out for him. "You can't go there, Marco. Please, don't do this. Whatever is going to happen, you probably can't stop it anyway."

"So, I just sit back and let it happen?"

"If you go there, you'll never come back out!"

"And if I stay, I'll never be able to live with myself!"

"There's no saving most of us, we're too damaged. And besides," she said, her voice becoming hard, "the men and women who did this to us don't deserve saving. Especially by you."

"Just like Dr. Brennan, right?"

"Yes, actually."

"And you? Did you deserve to be saved or left there? If I could've saved you, would it have been worth it?"

Delilah swallowed.

"I'm going," Marco said, "and you can either help me or not. Your choice."

"I can't go back there."

"I'm not asking you to. I just need to know if the information in that file is correct and if there's anything we're missing."

Delilah paused, and then opened the file folder. "I'll help you," she finally said, "because it's you, Marco. Because...I can't not help you."

Marco didn't even want to think about what that meant, so he simply nodded. "Thank you."

"Here..." she said, taking a chain out of her pocket. "I got it off Dr. Trace before he was taken away." The key dangled at the end of the chain like a small, fragile last hope. Marco stared at it.

"Hang on to it for me," he said.

Delilah frowned. "Why?"

"If I don't make it out, there's something I need you to do for me."

"What?"

Marco ran to the kitchen and scrounged until he found a piece of paper and pen. He jotted down Alice's address on one piece of paper, and a quick note on another.

"Send it here, with this," he said, handing both pieces of paper to her. "If I make it out tonight, I'll come to Allegra's before you leave tomorrow and get the key from you. And if I don't, you must promise me you'll send it to this address. Please?"

"Of course," she said, giving him a half smile. "But you *will* make it out. You have to."

He let her take his hand and give it a squeeze. For a moment he remembered last night, the naked passion they'd shared, and he wanted to kiss her, in spite of everything.

But, like last night, Delilah got there first. She reached up and pressed her lips to his, light and soft.

"For luck," she said.

The last thing Colleen wanted to do was watch the excruciating conversation that was about to take place between Delilah and Marco. Though, if she were honest with herself, seeing whatever surprise Tina had left in the trunk wasn't all that much better.

"Hey," Dante said just before she reached the back door, "what happened here today…"

"Yeah?"

"Is that the end of it? For this neighborhood, I mean."

"You're asking if Grandfather Malone is going to retaliate against you or these people?"

Dante nodded.

"No. Grandfather Malone is dead, and his next in line won't touch this place. You have my word."

He sagged with relief and sighed. "Thank you."

Colleen turned away, feeling a strange kind of power that had nothing to do with the fire she could summon. Tina had always insisted that if Colleen stood beside her, she'd get to do some good, fix things that Grandfather had destroyed. Colleen had always thought it was a ploy to get her to stay. But just now, having the power to reassure Dante that this place was safe…Colleen started to see what Tina might have meant all those years ago.

I'm not going to think of that right now. Maybe not ever. That decision…It might not end up like I think it will, just like everything else with my family. But I can help Andrew so…

She walked out to the car and stared at the trunk. It was ridiculous to be frightened of something that could fit inside a trunk, Colleen knew that. She also knew that there were very good reasons for her trepidations.

"Here we go," she said, unlocking and opening the trunk.

Inside was a dull black foot locker with a padlock and an envelope attached.

"The key is on the ring, smallest one."

Her hands shook a little as she unlocked the padlock and opened the lid.

And then, she laughed.

Nestled inside was a carefully folded and stored suit. And not just any kind of suit.

She grabbed the dark orange shirt, which was made of an odd, heavy material and held it up. A thrill shot through her spine, along with fear and a nervous energy that made her body grow hot.

Setting it back inside, Colleen took the envelope and opened it. In her mother's handwriting was another note.

"I know you may not think much of this power, but I do. Not for my benefit, but for others. You may not believe me, and that's fine. I have my plans and skills to make our corner of the world better here in High Tide, and I believe you do as well. How you choose to use that power is up to you. To that end, I commissioned this suit to be made. It's fire proof and reinforced in the torso and gloves to protect and aid you in a fight. The palms of the gloves are open to help you better manifest your powers, and the boots are specially designed to grip surfaces that might be slick due to the heat you generate. The fabric is also light enough to allow your skin to breath while also protecting you and not igniting from your powers. Whether you want to be a part of my world or not, please accept this and know that I believe in you, Tina."

Tears fell in fat drops onto the paper, smearing the black ink. A series of small sobs escaped her lips and she had to take deep gulping breaths to calm herself. There had been days, weeks, even months, when Colleen could not believe that her mother loved her. How could a woman who did the things Tina did, love anyone, really love them? And yet here was proof that at the very least her mother saw and respected her.

She stuffed the note into her pocket and closed the lid of the foot locker. It took a little doing to get it out of the trunk and into the back room of the gym. When she did, Colleen opened it once more and took a long look at what her mother had given her.

"I guess," she said with a smirk. "That I'm going to need a code name."

CHAPTER NINETEEN

Lumis was on the outskirts of Metro City, practically in another town. Home to an old wartime training facility, most of the old buildings had been cleared to make way for the enormous rectangular structure that was Lumis Labs.

A half mile from the ten feet tall electric fence at the back of the complex, stood sparse trees, while on the other sides were fields of tall winter grass. On the tree side of the complex, some of the old barracks had been left standing. To an outsider, it might appear that someone had been too lazy to tear them down. But in reality, it was a very purposeful decision to leave the six buildings standing.

Two of the barracks were used as storage for different kinds of equipment, one had two huge cold storage units on a separate power grid, in case the main power went out. Two others had various body bags, coffins, and transportation tubes for the "specimens" of the lab. And then, within the sixth building, an entrance had been carved into the concrete floor, where a staircase leading down into an underground tunnel system led to and from the secret lab where Lumis' true purposes were undertaken.

Marco and Colleen drove to the sparse grove of trees and parked the car on the bumpy dirt road hidden within the trees.They walked the half mile from the trees, and then pushed aside a broken part of the chain link fence behind the old barracks, just as several large trucks pulled through the main gates. Crouching down, they watched the line move forward, into the complex. The trucks bore the markings of a high-end moving company, easily seen as they pulled into a barely intact loading area at the back of the burned out Lumis facility.

Low lights illuminated a small parking lot that contained five or six cars, casting the fire damaged building in strange shadows. Frost glistened on the grass and hard brown earth, the sky overhead was clear with the barest sliver of moon hanging among the stars.

"The inside of the topside labs was the most damaged," Delilah had said. "They claimed structural damage to keep anyone from looking too close and discovering what was underneath, but the walls are still intact and secure. It all looks worse than it likely is."

Staring at the building now, Colleen could see what Delilah had meant. Windows gaped like vast black holes from the fire scarred walls, which were still standing, as was the roof. None of it compared to the devastation at the apartment building she'd burned down just a few days ago. Certainly not bad enough to forbid anyone from investigating.

Colleen looked down at the suit she was wearing and smiled. It was orange, a deep hue that reminded Colleen of flames. White piping ran up the outside of her thighs and arms, as well as the front and sides of her torso. A white domino mask clung to her face and hid her identity, she hoped.

Marco had asked her how she felt about the suit when

they were driving to Lumis and she'd been at a loss for words at first.

"Good," she finally said. "It feels good like...I don't have to hide in this."

Marco had nodded, as if he knew exactly what she'd meant and put his own domino mask on.

"What do I call you?" he'd asked before they got out of the car.

Colleen bit her lip, unsure about the name she'd picked. Finally, she took a deep breath and decided to just go with it.

"Call me...Fahrenheit."

Marco had smiled. "That's a good name."

Now they stood within the Lumis compound, ready to begin a mission that could kill them both.

Or make us lab experiments.

She shuddered at the thought and Marco looked at her with frown.

"You ready?" he asked.

"Yeah, let's do it."

"Remember, I'm Shadow Master," Marco asked, standing up, his duster swirling around his legs. "And don't worry if it's hard to remember your own code name in a fight. It took me months."

She nodded and they made their way to the barrack with the underground entrance.

According to Tina's information, it would normally be guarded with surveillance cameras and guards positioned at certain points. But the fire had damaged a few of the electrical systems, and they hadn't bothered to repair the one that powered the security cameras. The problem, of course, was that the lights didn't work either. They stared into a deep hole of darkness once the hatch was opened.

"I got it," Colleen said, taking a deep breath and creating a small ball of flame.

True to Tina's word, the suit didn't burst into flames as the ball sat in her palm.

They descended the staircase that ended at the beginning of a wide hallway. As they walked, the hallway began to have a definite downward slant and Colleen felt her heart beat quicken. Never having gone into an underground tunnel that led to a nefarious lab, Colleen had no way of knowing that she'd feel panicked.

"Hey," Marco said, stopping her with a hand on her arm. "It's okay."

The flame grew in her palm, and then shrank down.

"Use your powers on me," she said, her breath starting to come in quick gasps.

Marco hesitated.

"If you don't, and I lose control in here…"

Long tendrils of shadow curled around her, and Colleen began to second guess her request. But after a moment, her breathing evened out and she felt peace like a wave course through her. She looked at Marco to thank him and stopped, mouth open. His eyes were completely black and the shadows swirled around him.

"Let's go," he said, his eyes turning back to normal.

Colleen nodded, concentrating on the flame in her hand.

"I had no idea," she said after a few minutes.

"Does it make a difference?" he asked.

"No. You're you, and these powers…we didn't ask for them, but we'll use them best we can, right?"

Marco looked at her, a tender expression on his masked face. "Right."

The hallway had become level now and a faint light could be seen in the distance, possibly marking the end of the hallway, which seemed to go on forever. Colleen felt her body hum with energy as they finally drew near the dim light and she extinguished the flame in her palm.

She had memorized the blueprints of the underground

lab in a few minutes, something that she had always been able to do, and knew that there would be a door at the end of this hallway that led to a small side hallway.

The closer they got, the brighter the light became until she worried they might be exposed if someone was waiting there. Soon though, they could see the door that would lead them into the lab and it was, to her relief, not guarded.

It was, however, locked.

Marco stepped in front of her, took a small case from his pocket and began to pick the lock.

Colleen chuckled. "So that's how you got into so much trouble."

He grinned. "It's handy for both vigilantism and private investigating."

The lock soon popped open and he looked up at her. She held his gaze for a moment, and nodded in response to his unspoken question.

I'm ready. I can do this. We can do this.

He stepped through first, as the more experienced person in this sort of thing. The hallway was deserted, an eerie silence hanging in the air. Marco closed his eyes, shadows seeping out of his fingertips and hovering in the air.

"No one near," he said, opening his now blackened eyes. "But…further down…to the right…."

Colleen nodded. "We have to pass six hallways, three on each side. The one on the right after that will be the containment cells, the one on the left will lead to the main lab."

Marco led the way and Colleen followed him down the hall. The lighting was minimal, as if it were dimmed for the night shift. The further they went the more Colleen was able to hear quiet voices and the rattle of something that could be a stretcher.

A stretcher that probably has a powered person strapped to it.

The thought made her jaw clench and her blood go

molten under skin. And, to her shock and for the first time in her life, Colleen wasn't afraid of it. Instead, she welcomed it. This was how she would make a difference in her world, how she'd save Andrew, and protect those who couldn't protect themselves.

This is who I am. And I'm done hiding it.

Her vision became bright, like it had earlier that day. Instead of it happening because she was losing control, Colleen knew it was because she was starting to embrace the power inside of her.

They were a few feet from what would've been the hallway leading to the containment cells when a man in a lab coat turned the corner from the left hallway. When he saw the two of them, his face registered fear and shock. Before he could get out a warning, Marco's shadows wrapped around him and he dropped to the ground, eyes closed.

Colleen knew that he'd soon be discovered, but there wasn't time to drag him off somewhere.

Suddenly, shouts came from the left, toward the main lab, followed by screams of panic.

"Liam," Marco said, turning to Colleen. "You go find your brother, I'll handle him."

She nodded. "Meet you back at the entrance of the tunnel."

Marco ran off to the left and she went to the right, then took the first left to a hall ending with a thick security door.

Two guards stood outside, stun guns at the ready. Colleen didn't hesitate, she threw a fireball straight at their feet, then manipulated it so it encircled them.

The two men stared up at her, eyes wide through the flames. One of them raised a stun gun as if to fire at her, but Colleen was now near enough to punch him in the face and take the gun from him.

Recalling the flames to her, she grabbed the gun from

209

the second guard and delivered a jab to his solar plexus. He doubled over and she slammed her knee into his face. He fell to the ground, still hot from her flames, blood splattered over his face.

The other guard had recovered from his shock enough to punch Colleen in the side. She felt her muscles contract and gasped. He was behind and to the side of her, so Colleen drove her elbow into his face, then delivered two quick punches to his mid-section. He sprawled backward onto the floor and she kicked him across the face.

Both guards were now unconscious. Colleen knew there wasn't time to find something to tie them up with, so she dragged them further down the hall, away from the cells, and stuffed them in a utility closet. Praying the keycard her mother procured would work, Colleen ran back to the security door. It swung open just as a buzzing alarm sounded.

I don't think that's a good sign.

Trying to push away the sense of dread invading her mind, Colleen ran down the hall and skidded to a stop as she reached the row of containment cells.

The blueprints had shown three different sections down this hall, with a dozen cells in each section, six on each side, each section divided by a security door. This first section was where those with especially dangerous or hard to control powers were kept.

And every single cell door was open.

Though Colleen wasn't afraid of her brother, she had no idea what to expect from powered people who'd been conditioned into weapons.

With slow, careful steps she walked to the first two cells. Both were empty. She eased forward to the next ones, as people started wandering from the remaining cells. Some looked around with eyes full of fear and froze in the doorways, as if trained not to walk past that invisible barrier.

Others looked down the hall and took off running, their bare feet patting on the linoleum past Colleen. They seemed far too excited at the prospect of escape to do anything to her.

The buzzing alarm filled the hallway and Colleen almost missed a hissing sound behind her. She spun around and stared at a young woman that squatted just inside the doorway of a cell dressed in absolutely nothing. Scales covered her entire body, and the only evidence that she was female were two small breasts on her green and yellow chest, as well as the lack of something between the legs. Her feet were webbed, as were her fingers, which ended in sharp claws. She stared up at Colleen with eyes that had vertical slits in the center.

"I'm not going to hurt you," Colleen said, trying to infuse far more confidence in it than she felt.

The woman didn't seem to hear her at first, just tilted her head to the side. Then, in a blink of an eye, she sprang up, leaping on Colleen, a shrieking cry escaping her chapped lips.

Before Colleen could do anything, the woman clamped down on Colleen's neck with her sharp teeth.

Colleen screamed, more in panic than pain and let instinct take over. Heat pulsed out from her palms and into the woman, who screeched and jumped off Colleen, landing in a squatting position by the main security door.

The place where the woman bit Colleen was throbbing. She reached up to touch it and her fingers came away wet with blood.

The woman hissed again and shifted, as if ready to spring again.

Colleen let fire fill her hands, not wanting to hurt the poor lizard girl but not having much of a choice.

Just as the woman was readying to jump, a bolt of something white and cold shot past Colleen from behind and slammed into lizard girl. She keened, her scaled body writhing on the floor.

Colleen spun around, readying a fire ball, when she saw who had helped her. Stumbling forward, clad in a hospital nightgown, his face bruised and cut, was Andrew.

"Get out of here, you freak!" he shouted at the woman. "Before I freeze you to the floor."

Lizard girl rolled over and bounded away.

"Andrew?" Colleen said, eyes filling with tears. "You're alive!"

Even though they were far from safe and sound, it was as if a weight she hadn't been aware of was lifted off her, and she threw her arms around him. He was too thin, and he winced at the contact, as if his whole body hurt. When she pulled back, tears made tracks down Andrew's cheeks.

"I thought I was going to die in here..." His voice broke.

Screams echoed from behind him, and the sound of something banging against the wall.

"We still might, if we don't get out of here," she said, a sudden sharp pain shooting down her arm.

"Oh my god, she bit you!"

"Yeah, that was—"

"It's poisonous," he said, pulling Colleen to a first aid box on the wall.

"They have anti-venom in a first aid kit?" she asked, as pain lanced through her chest.

"In this place, they've got everything in the damn first aid kit."

Snarls and screams sounded a few feet away and Colleen turned to see three people lurching toward them. One was covered in golden fur, like a lion, his face still human, but wild. When he opened his mouth, unnaturally long canines dripped with saliva. Another was white as fresh paper, her long blue hair falling in unnatural curls to the floor, Colleen swore she saw the tendrils of hair twitch of their own accord.

Or maybe that's the poison.

Her vision was starting to go and her arm was becoming numb.

"How's that...going?" she asked.

"There's a lot of crap in here," he said, sifting through sets of syringes with numbers on them.

Colleen turned up the heat of her power.

"Maybe I can...burn some of it...Hey, is she floating?"

"Damn it," Andrew said, shooting knives of ice at the powered people. "These three! We need to go!"

He grabbed the first aid kit and pulled Colleen after him.

"Fire, as much as you can!"

She tried, unable to feel her right arm, so she used her left to lob sloppy fireballs at the three coming toward them. Her brother shot ice in quick succession, and the steam made it impossible for the three to see Colleen and Andrew.

"Fire, shoot it up, at the sprinklers!" he shouted, lobbing more ice knives into the thick steam.

Spots began appearing in her vision, but Colleen managed to shoot a stream of fire upwards. In moments, the sprinkler system activated, and the security doors began to shut. A new alarm sounded, this one more like a siren.

She half-stumbled toward the main security door, her brother pulling and shoving. They slid past the security door just before it closed.

Andrew grabbed Colleen's hand and pressed it to the handle and lock.

"Heat, not a lot just enough to melt it a little."

It took a few tries, but she managed it, just before something snarling and furry slammed into the door.

"I-I think...I need..." Colleen said, black creeping up the sides of her vision before sliding to the floor.

Andrew pulled a syringe with a thick yellow liquid from inside the first aid kit.

"This is going to hurt," he said, shoving the needle into the poisoned bite.

Colleen gasped, the liquid unbearably cold.

"N-No...no..." she gasped, her body starting to shake.

"I know – it's horrible," Andrew said, tossing the needle aside. "But it will neutralize the poison."

For the first time since she was twelve, Colleen couldn't feel that constant heat in her veins and panic took over.

"M-my power?" she whispered.

"Oh that..." Andrew's expression changed in an instant.

Gone was the concerned brother who needed rescuing. The angular planes of his face that she knew so well, the large brown eyes that had always been so gentle...it all hardened, cold and hate-filled.

"It's a temporary side effect. Didn't I mention it?" he asked, standing up. "You're powerless, at my mercy. Just like Grandfather was at the mercy of Tina."

Colleen gasped, edging away from Andrew.

"That's right," he nodded, "I know he's dead and I know who killed him. The Warden, that's what we called the man in charge of our group of cells, he kept me well informed. And do you know why?"

"N-no..." she said, teeth clacking together.

The cold was making her muscles cramp, as if she were immersed in a tub of ice.

Don't panic! Can't panic, gotta stay calm! Gotta think!

"Because I volunteered, that's why," Andrew continued. "I was here willingly to understand these gifts. I didn't run away like you did, didn't try to hide who I was and what I had to offer to Grandfather. I was loyal! Unlike you! You, the good one, the one he loved—"

"H-he d-didn't love anyone!"

Andrew back-handed her, and for a moment, Colleen felt a surge of heat run through her body.

"That's a lie!" Andrew said. "He would've loved *me*, if you and Tina hadn't made him think I was weak. Well, look at me *now*, big Sis!" He held his arms out and the rich brown skin became blue, frost crystals glittering along the surface like tiny diamonds in the low light.

Colleen watched as a long knife of ice grew in his hand. He squatted in front of her, cold coming off him in waves.

"See?" he said, his voice hoarse, sharp, like cracking ice. "I'm strong, powerful. More than you ever were."

"R-Really?" she said, an idea forming in her cloudy mind. "Y-you think some i-ice will make a difference? Y-you never c-could do the hard s-stuff."

"Like what?" he asked.

"L-like hurting someone...r-really hurting them."

Andrew's icy blue eyes blazed.

"Y-you were always too nice," Colleen said, trying her best to infuse the last word with disgust. "K-kill someone quick to get the p-pain over...r-remember? You couldn't... couldn't torture...not really. Not like me."

"Is that right?" he asked.

The icy tip of the knife dug into her cheek and she gasped as he cut a thin line under each cheekbone. The same surge of heat as before flared and Colleen's mind cleared, just a little.

"Pathetic," she said, doing her best to look at him like Grandfather would.

"You're wearing too many layers to—"

"Excuses!"

Andrew growled and punched her across the face.

If flesh on flesh hurt, getting hit with a fist of ice was enough to make Colleen wonder if she was going to be knocked unconscious. Pain exploded from her jaw to her cheek and into her eye. And along with pain, heat, glorious and strong.

Just a little more.

"That all?" she said.

Andrew punched her again, this time on the other side. Colleen tasted blood and felt fire in her veins. Her mind was still a little foggy, though she didn't know if that was the drug or the fact that two blocks of ice had crashed into her head.

Gotta time it just right.

"How about that?" he yelled, his strange voice cracking. "You want more?"

The ice fist careened toward her again and Colleen dodged at the last minute. Her brother's fist smashed into the wall and he let out a gruesome howl of pain.

"No, I'm good thanks," she said, letting the little heat she could channel into her bare palms as she pressed her hands to her brother's icy skin.

Steam rose off of him and he screamed again. She started to move to the side and he back-handed her. The force of the hit knocked her off balance and she fell. Andrew came at her again, ice shooting out of his hands. Colleen rolled away and stumbled to her feet. Her muscles still felt weak, as if she'd run for miles up hill.

The fire is coming back, I just need to get a little more...

"You gonna fight me?" Andrew said. "Without your powers?"

"I never needed powers to win a fight," she said, delivering a punch to Andrew's midsection.

And immediately regretted it.

Andrew laughed as she shook her hand in pain. "Like hitting a block of ice, isn't it, Sis?"

Colleen glared at him. "I always thought you'd grow out of being a little shit. But I guess I was wrong."

"Can't take being bested by me?"

"Bested? Please," she said, pushing all the heat she could into her hands. "Fire beats ice every time."

Colleen punched him across the face, then two quick jabs to the gut. Even though the heat in her hands mitigated the feel of Andrew's ice skin, the impact still hurt. It was working though, so she kept at it. Steam rose up in a hissing cloud, and Andrew fell back against the wall. His blue skin was fading, but not completely gone.

More heat began to build in her veins and Colleen pushed just a little more into her fists, punching Andrew once again in the face, the bones of his nose crunching under her knuckles. Her mind recoiled from the knowledge that she'd just broken her brother's nose and she stepped back.

"I'm sorry, Andrew," she said as her brother's skin once again became brown. "I wish...I wish you hadn't loved that old lunatic so much."

"And I wish you weren't so weak," he said.

Even though her powers were returning, Colleen's body was still slow from the poison and antidote. She saw the ice knives fly from her brothers fingers a second too late to dodge all of them. One knife sliced into her side and landed behind her. The other impaled itself into her forearm. She stared at the ice shard as it melted, blood and water pooling at her feet. Colleen felt her head swim with the pain pulsing in her arm and side.

Andrew laughed from where he still sat on the floor. "Fire beats ice, huh?"

Anger, quick and raging, overwhelmed Colleen and she charged at her brother. He raised his hands as if to shoot more ice knives at her, and never got the chance. Colleen punched him twice, as hard as she could, in the face, and he collapsed in a heap.

"I'll come back for you, idiot," she said, clutching her injured arm.

It was bleeding enough that she'd be too weak to be much help in a little while.

There's one thing I can do...

Colleen bit down on a scream as she stuck her fingers into the hole left by the ice knife. Taking several gulping breaths, she forced all the heat she could into her fingers. Pain, such as she'd never experienced, consumed her and she screamed, a deep, fierce sound.

Her knees buckled and she fell to the floor, vision wavering.

Don't pass out...don't pass out!

She concentrated on breathing, slow and deep. As she did, Colleen eased her fingers out of the now cauterized wound. Taking a few more breaths, Colleen forced herself to her feet and stumbled toward the main area where Marco had gone.

The center of the underground lab was a sunken circular room, where large computers took up half the circle on the left, controlling everything from individual containment cells, to keeping track of data from experiments and missions. Every piece of information was stored in the computers and backed up in the huge filing cabinets that took up a quarter of the circle on the right. Next to the filing cabinets were surgical tables, stretchers, and all kinds of medical equipment. In the center of the circular room was a large space reserved for special viewings of new drugs or enhancements, or large meetings.

The hallway that ran next to the room was dimly lit, but Marco could see bodies lying throughout, some dressed in lab coats, others in guard uniforms.

When he peeked around the doorway to the room, he could see Liam perched on top of a table, the Six Man next to him, and another powered person, a woman with a wide grin on her too thin face. They were dressed in mover's coveralls and Marco realized that they'd probably killed the real movers and gotten in through the loading dock at the opposite end of the facility.

Killing as they went.

A woman lay on the table on the right side of the circular room, sobbing as a greenish liquid was injected into her by a man in a lab coat. The man's movements were jerky, just like Allegra's had been, and Marco knew that Liam was controlling him.

"Please," the woman begged. "I'm so sorry!"

Liam wandered over to her and grinned. "What's my name? My real name?"

The woman frowned.

"That's what I thought," he said.

"Wait! I can remember if you just-Ah!"

She thrashed around on the table, arching her back.

"Come now," Liam said, walking away, "it can't hurt that bad."

Marco was about to let his shadows loose on Liam when suddenly Marco was hit from behind, hard enough to send him flying through the doorway and into the room, crashing into two office chairs.

He blinked away the stars in his vision and looked up in time to see a blur of movement, and then something hit him in the stomach hard enough to send him flying into the chairs. For a moment, Marco couldn't breathe and he choked on bile rising in the back of his throat.

"Wait!" Liam yelled.

A woman stood over him, brown hair lank and covering half her long face, a loose pair of hospital scrubs hung on her thin frame. Behind her was a body, the head snapped unnaturally to one side, another one lying beside it. The woman on the table gave another guttural cry, and then collapsed onto the table, her eyes staring at nothing though Marco could still see her chest rise and fall.

"Well," Liam continued, "I was hoping you'd join the party. Everyone, this is my best friend…what do I call you? Shadow Master or Marco?"

Marco spat out some of the bile in his mouth and tried to sit up. "Call me whatever the hell you like."

"How considerate, giving me a choice. Now, Miss Lang," Liam said, turning to a small woman sitting in absolute terror by a nearby computer, "disable the fail safes, all the locks to every door. And don't forget the outside alarm system."

The woman shook as she reached over and began typing on the keyboard in front of her. In moments, an alarm began to buzz overhead.

"She set off an alarm!" the fast woman said.

Liam held a knife out to Miss Lang. "Take it."

The woman cried, but took the hilt of the knife. "I-It's not my fault! Th-there's back door systems, I'm just a secondary programmer! Please!"

"Where does the alarm go to? Check it!"

She did, holding the knife in one hand as she typed with the other. "An outside system…I-I don't know where."

"Now…" Liam began.

Marco had been gathering his shadows as Liam talked and now he let them loose on the woman, trying his best over ride Liam's control. Shadows swirled around her, cocooning her in darkness. Marco wasn't gentle, he didn't have time. He yanked open the door of her mind and grabbed the first thing he found that would be awful enough. She gave a strangled cry and fell from the chair, an unconscious heap on the floor.

The fast woman struck Marco across the face hard enough to make him taste blood.

"Pointless," Liam said, "she'll be dead no matter what you do. Now? Later? It's only a matter of time."

"Can I take care of this ass?" the fast woman asked.

"No Lisa, let him stay."

"But—"

"She was very specific! She doesn't want us hurting each other if we can help it. Besides, Marco will come around, you'll see."

Lisa backed off, her face going pale.

Whoever 'she' is, it's someone bad enough to scare her just with a mention. I've got to find out who it is, and his obsession with bringing me into the fold might be the ticket.

Liam looked toward the door as someone leapt through it. She was naked, covered in green and yellow iridescent scales, like a reptile. Her deep green eyes had vertical slits in them, and she crouched on the table like a frog.

"Ah, Julia," Liam said. "I was hoping you'd still be here."

Julia hissed in response.

"Who is 'she'?" Marco asked, standing up.

Liam turned to him and smiled. "You'll find out soon, my friend. She's the best of us, the one who'll make a world where none of us will ever be afraid again. You'll see."

"What if I don't want to?"

The woman on the table began to cry, a hoarse, primal sound that chilled Marco's blood. He wondered if he could end it, the way he had with Miss Lang, when the buzzing alarms were replaced with something that sounded more like a siren. By the look on Liam's face, Marco guessed this wasn't part of his plan.

Taking advantage of the diversion, Marco let his vision go gray again and he shot the shadows out toward the man injecting the solution. Marco was aware of Liam screaming at him to stop, and a whoosh of air as Lisa ran toward him, but his focus was on the man's mind. It was sloppy and quick as he pulled a horrible memory to the man's mind and amplified it.

The man screamed and fell to his knees, Marco felt a powerful jab to his stomach and almost lost the connection. He held on through sheer force of will until the man was unconscious, and then jumped to the woman.

A punch to Marco's face and his vision wavered back to normal. He grit his teeth and tried to push into the woman's mind when fists slammed into him from all sides and he lost control of the shadows.

Blood was dripping off his nose when Marco opened his eyes and saw the Six Man standing above him.

"Hey," all the copies said together, "remember me?"

"Wish...I didn't."

Another fist careened toward his face and Marco felt blood burst in his mouth.

"Enough," Liam said.

Marco spat blood on the floor and gasped as he tried to get up. His stomach was on fire, and the muscles of his back protested at every movement.

Liam turned around and looked at one of the Six Man copies. "Will the fire alarm keep the rest from escaping?"

"Probably."

Liam swore. "Time to leave then."

The sound of booted feet running reached them under the screeching of the newest alarm. Marco looked toward the door to see at least six guards in black gear, wearing chest pieces that looked reinforced, with strange-looking guns in their hands. They lined up in formation just outside the circular room.

"Stand down now!" said one of the men.

"I thought you took care of the guards," Liam said to Lisa.

"The outside alarm must've called some in. How'd they get here so fast?"

Liam sighed. "Give me cover."

Six Man and all his copies walked in front of Liam as they approached the doorway.

Marco knew what was about to happen. Even if saving the guards resulted in his possible incarceration, he couldn't let Liam control and kill them.

He reached out with his powers, but not toward the Six Man or Liam. Instead he focused on Lisa, brushing against her mind with subtle feathers of power. She twitched, as if someone had run a finger down her spine. He didn't wait for her to figure out what was about to happen.

With lightning speed, his shadows rolled out of him and latched onto Lisa. She didn't have a moment to scream, her mouth hanging open as Marco opened the door of her mind. He saw so many options, so much pain and fear, but he needed a particularly nasty one to make it quick. It felt like he lingered far too long searching, when in reality it was just a few seconds. What he found made bile rise to Marco's throat for the second time that night, and with a cringe, he pulled on it, bringing it to the fore, giving it power.

Lisa did scream now, raw and terrible. Her body convulsed and she fell to the floor, sobbing.

The world was still a silver gray when the lizard girl, Julia, launched herself at him. He wrapped his shadows around her and—

What...? What is this?

Where there should have been a house, or something at least resembling it, there was nothing. Just a tangle of vines and trees, dark and ancient.

Sharp claws dragged down the protective armor on his chest, snapping him out of her mind. He stumbled back, the shock of not finding anything to latch onto in her memories disorienting him. She swiped his legs out and jumped on top of him. In the back of his mind, Marco felt keen discomfort touching a naked woman's chest the way he was, but mostly he was just trying to keep her sharp teeth from sinking into his flesh.

He pressed his right forearm into her throat and punched Julia in the stomach with his left fist. She gave a gurgling cough and scampered off him. Marco stood, his face and body throbbing from the blows he'd received.

Julia crouched, her cold stare boring into him as she prepared to strike once more.

The guards started to yell, and as they fired, Marco realized that they were no longer holding stun guns. This was live ammo.

Marco picked up one of the crappy office chairs and threw it at Julia as she leapt at him. He took off running toward the guards.

Julia snarled behind him and threw the chair to side, leaping over tables on all fours. Marco turned, ready to defend himself when a ball of fire shot past him and slammed into Julia, who shrieked as she collapsed to the floor. The fireball retreated off the lizard girl before too much damage had been done, leaving her skin dark and peeling.

The Six Man was also gone, or at least his copies were. A stray bullet must've found the real Man, because he was laying on the floor, his chest soaked in blood, vacant eyes staring up.

Marco reached Liam, who was taking cover behind a pushed over table and punched his face. His thin frame fell to the floor, dark eyes hard as he looked at Marco.

"You idiot!" Liam said. "They'll kill you, too!"

Marco punched Liam again. "This isn't the way."

Fire erupted between the guards and the doorway. A few of the guards who had been about to step into the room fell back, screaming from burns.

"At least someone knows what to do," Liam stood up, wiping blood from his mouth.

"She's not killing them," Marco said.

"Marco!" Colleen said from outside the room. "I can't hold this long. I'll try to move them back, give you a chance to get out."

Bullets pinged outside the room and Colleen swore.

"I'm flanked!"

"Let me out!" Marco said, running to the door.

There was barely enough space for him to squeeze out without getting burned, but he did it. Running around to the left of the doorway and down the hall, he passed Colleen and released his shadows.

The group of men in dark uniforms, were readying their guns to fire. Marco didn't have the time to manipulate them one by one.

There is one thing I can do...

He'd done it once before, at Park Side, and if it hadn't been for Alice and Lionel, he'd have lost control completely. After what Liam had done to him, and the difficulty he'd been having lately controlling the shadows, his heart was pounding at the thought of doing anything that would make him truly lose control.

One of the men fired, missing Marco and Colleen by inches.

If I don't, we'll die...I can do this, I have to.

Taking a deep breath, Marco let the world go silver-gray and this time he pushed on his powers, driving the shadows from his body in a rushing torrent. In seconds, he had built them up into a cyclone around the men. He couldn't see clearly enough for nuance, all he could do was take the emotions, in this case their extreme hatred and fear, and drain it. As the shadows spun and writhed faster, he could hear some of the men scream, and felt like joining them. The sheer volume of what he was taking fell in waves on Marco's mind and he groaned, shoving it away as quickly as he could.

A primal instinct urged him to go on, to take more. Just a little push here or there and those men would be broken forever, never able to harm anyone, ever again.

It's clean, simple. I can admit that now. But it's not me, I won't let it be me.

Marco expected it to be difficult to call the shadows back, but all it took was a tug and they obeyed, rolling in a great wave back to him. The men were left lying in a heap, unconscious.

Marco swayed, falling against the nearest wall. Aftertaste was too mild a word to describe what was left behind from these men. It consumed him, soaking his mind and soul in the disgust and hate they felt.

We really are animals to them...we aren't human...

"Shadow!" Colleen yelled as more gunfire erupted.

Something slammed into him just as bullets lodged themselves into the wall where he'd been standing.

"Hey," she said, tapping him on the face. "Look at me."

When he did, the world was still silver-gray, and Colleen jerked back from him. He forced his vision back to normal and saw her for the first time since they had parted ways. Both her cheeks had dried blood on them from twin cuts just below her cheekbones, her bottom lip was swollen, and her left eye looked like it would become a wicked shiner. When she helped him up, he noticed how she favored one arm, and saw the dried blood covering the forearm and evidence of a jagged wound.

"Are you alright?"

"I'll live. C'mon," she ordered, "we need to get out of here."

A voice sounded on the speakers, crisp and emotionless: "Countermeasures deployed in five minutes. Poison gas release in five minutes."

She swore and helped Marco to his feet.

"One of the guards must've done it." he said, forcing the leftover feelings away enough to think clearly.

"They couldn't contain us so they'll just trap and kill us."

They looked at each other at the same time.

"The door!"

"Andrew..." Colleen said. "I have to make sure—" She took off in the opposite direction of the door that would take them to the only exit they knew.

"Fahrenheit, wait!"

"I'll meet you there!"

Marco started to run toward their exit when someone tackled him from behind and he fell to the floor.

"You ruined it all!" Liam shrieked, pummeling Marco with his fists. "Now I'll die here because of you!"

Liam was sitting low on Marco's stomach, so he brought his leg up and around Liam, forcing him to the ground. At the same time, he grabbed Liam's arm and trapped it between his legs, pulling on it just enough so that the muscles started to strain.

"Stop fighting me!" Marco said. "You don't have to die here, you can come with us!"

"And then what? You'll turn me over to a nut house?"

"I don't know! But if you won't let me go, we both will die here."

Liam glared at him, but Marco could tell he was getting through. He took a chance, released Liam and stood up.

"Come with me," Marco held his hand. "Prove them wrong. Show them you're not a monster."

Liam hesitated, then took Marco's hand.

"You trust me?" Liam asked.

"No. Not yet."

Liam shook his head. "You know—" The bullet hit Liam

just under his collar bone, pitching him forward and into Marco.

"Stand down!" a guard said, walking with hesitation toward them.

There were two of them, both pointing their guns at Marco with cold intensity in their eyes. He knew what was in their hearts, the ruthless determination and belief that people like him, like Liam, deserved to be put down like dogs.

Marco clenched his jaw and let his shadows have their lead. One of the men got another shot off before he was too overcome with terror to do much other than scream. The bullet grazed Marco's bicep, a fiery slice of pain that he ignored.

It was quick work to make the two guards blubbering puddles on the floor.

"Three minutes until countermeasures are deployed. Three minutes until poison gas release."

I just condemned them to death...and I don't think I care.

The knowledge chilled him, and he wanted to do something when Liam gasped in his arms.

"Please..." he said, his chest covered in blood. "Don't let me ...die here."

"Shadow...what...?" Colleen ran up to them, staring at Liam.

"Help me carry him."

Colleen put one of Liam's arms around her neck while Marco did the same with the other. He was so short that when they stood up his feet dangled a few inches above the ground.

"Andrew?" Marco asked, as they ran for the way out.

Colleen's face tightened. "I couldn't find him where I'd left him and...It's a long story."

They made it to the door, but when Colleen pulled on

the handle it wouldn't budge. She tried the key card, and it only buzzed at her.

"No!" she yelled.

"The hinges," Marco said "Melt them."

"I'm not sure I can. I'm feeling weak and my powers... I've never used them this much."

"Try."

Colleen took a deep breath and put her hands on the hinges of the door. Heat was obviously radiating from her palms but the metal didn't do anything.

"You can do this," Marco said. "You're stronger than you think you are."

She grunted, arms shaking with the effort.

"Damn it...melt the damn hinges...Now!" Liam said, his weak voice infused with command.

Colleen's spine jerked up a little and within moments the hinges began to glow, then the metal became soft under her hands and the hinges fell at her feet.

Marco helped Colleen pry the door open and the two of them once again picked up Liam.

"You realize," Colleen said, her breath coming in large gulps, "that because of what I did, the door won't seal the gas inside? We will have to get away from here, fast."

Marco nodded, and then remembered that she wouldn't be able to see him as the tunnel became increasingly dark. Soon, their quick breathing and desperate footsteps were the only sound as they raced up the incline that would lead them to the barracks and outside.

Liam groaned, and Marco knew that the way they were jostling him, Liam was likely in a lot of pain.

"Almost there," he said.

"Okay," he replied, his voice faint.

It felt as if the tunnel went on and on in the dark. Any minute now Marco expected the thick gas to come rolling toward them, bringing death.

Almost there, we have to be.

Finally, Marco saw the stairs by the dim light of the entrance and breathed a sigh of relief. He picked Liam up in his arms, the stairs too narrow for the three of them to walk side by side, and prayed that this door wouldn't be locked as well.

Colleen reached it first and shoved it open.

"This might be enough to hold the gas in," Colleen said closing the door once Marco and Liam were out.

"Let's not take any chances," Marco said.

Colleen nodded and helped him with Liam, who looked like he would soon pass out.

They got to the car without incident and drove as fast as possible down the dirt road until they hit the main road. Colleen floored it and they headed toward Metro City.

Marco sat in the back, with Liam laying across the back seat. His chest rose and fell in an erratic pattern.

He won't survive much longer.

Colleen glanced back and said, "There's a hospital in High Tide. Not great, but it would be the first one we could get to."

Marco was about to tell her to do it when Liam interrupted.

"No...hospital."

"You need help."

Liam's eyes opened part way and he gave Marco a weak smile. "Too late for that...old friend."

"No," Marco leaned over, putting his hand over Liam's. "We can make this right."

Liam gave his head a little shake. "I used to love... looking at the stars when dad would...take us camping. Not many stars in...the city. Are there stars...tonight?"

Marco looked out of the window and saw that the sky was still cold and clear.

"Colleen, pull over."

She hesitated, and then did so.

"There's a blanket in the trunk," she said. "You want me to…"

"No," Marco said.

She nodded, keeping her eyes ahead.

Marco felt his chest tighten as he got the blanket and threw it over Liam's pale body. Blood had seeped onto the back seat, and was smeared on Marco's duster.

So much blood. It won't be long.

As he carried Liam through a wide field of short winter grass, covered in delicate frost that glistened in the moonlight, Marco wondered if he could have done anything to save Liam from all this. If he'd been stronger, if he'd been able to capture Liam back at the apartment building.

"Not your fault," Liam said, as if reading Marco's mind.

He looked down at his pale face, the bright, dark eyes.

"I chose this," Liam continued. "My choice…finally, something that was…my choice."

Tears burned Marco's eyes as they stopped in the middle of the field. Liam looked up and smiled. Marco did the same. Overhead the sky was vibrant with stars twinkling in the inky black sea of a winter night sky.

"Beautiful," Liam whispered after a few minutes. "Thank you."

Marco swallowed as tears began to course down his face.

"Liam, I'm so sorry," he said.

When he looked down at Liam, his eyes were closed, face relaxed, peaceful. Marco looked to see if Liam's chest rose and fell at all, but it was still.

"I'm sorry," he whispered again, more tears falling in cold tracks down his cheeks.

His steps were heavy as he made his way back to the car. With the gentleness he would have used with a child,

Marco placed Liam in the back seat, covering him completely with the blanket.

"I'm so sorry, Marco. Is there anything…"

"No. Thank you," he said, sliding into the back seat with Liam's body.

She nodded and pulled back onto the main road.

They didn't speak the rest of the drive back.

CHAPTER TWENTY

Colleen knew the only place she could take them was her mother's office. There was always someone there in case of emergencies, so when she pulled into the alley beside the old theater, one of Tina's burly guards stepped out of the shadows to find out what was going on.

Colleen and Marco walked up the steps to the office, her arm and face throbbing in pain. Marco was battered and bloodied as well, his face cut and bruised, and he walked like his back and stomach had been worked over.

The minute they stepped into the office and Tina saw them, she swore, running from behind the desk. It shouldn't have been surprising to find Tina actually at the theater, waiting to find out what happened.

However, it was a shock when Tina went straight to Colleen and reached out, as if to embrace her. Colleen stepped back on instinct, then regretted it when Tina's face fell for a split second. Drawing herself up and putting on her usual stern face, Tina looked Colleen over and swore again when she saw her arm.

"I'll call our doctor," Tina said, walking back to her phone.

"And the mortician," Colleen said, peeling the cowl off her face and letting it hang behind her.

Tina stopped, shoulders sagging. "So, he was…"

"Not Andrew," Colleen said. "Someone else. No one can know."

Tina nodded, her face showing hints of relief as she dialed the phone. When she'd finished speaking to whoever was on the other end, she went straight to her sideboard and poured three generous glasses of scotch.

"You don't have to tell me details now," Tina said, pouring each of them a glass of Scotch, "but I assume since Andrew isn't with you that he's-"

"Tomorrow," Colleen said, her throat tight.

Tina nodded. "You can have the Brights apartment for the night, if you'd like."

Colleen stopped mid-drink.

The Brights apartment was what her mother had used to entertain out of town guests, who were used to a certain amount of luxury. A large three-bedroom apartment in the upper East side of Metro City, everyone assumed it was her primary residence, but Tina preferred the small brownstone that she'd grown up in.

"Thank you," Colleen said.

"I need to get to Delilah," Marco said.

"After the doctor has had a look at you," Tina said, her voice firm.

"It's nothing I haven't—"

"Mr. Mayer, I insist."

Marco paused, meeting Tina's dark gaze before nodding. "But I have to be able to get to her before the morning."

"Of course, it shouldn't take long."

They sat in silence thick with what had transpired that night. Colleen couldn't keep her brother's cold gaze out of her mind.

He hates me.

She flinched from the thought, and took a drink of Scotch. If Andrew wanted to live this way, there was nothing she could do about it. He was on his own now, and he would find out soon what it meant to be alone.

If he survived the gas.

Tears filled her eyes and slid down her cheeks before she could stop them, and she brushed them away with the back of her hand.

If I'd been here, if I could've talked with him, made him see…

She shook her head, trying to dislodge the thoughts.

"Stop it," Tina said. Colleen looked up and met her mother's narrowed eyes. "He made his own choice," Tina continued, her voice rough. "Neither one of us could protect him from that old man."

"Maybe we only made it worse."

"Maybe. One thing is certain though – neither one of us can do a damn thing to change it now."

"So, that's it?" Colleen asked. "We just give up and walk away?"

"You want to wallow, you go right ahead. I didn't do it when you left, and I'm not gonna start doing it now."

Colleen stared at her mother with wide eyes, her mouth hanging open. "And here I thought you actually cared about your children," she said, getting to her feet.

"Where you going?" Tina asked.

"I'm not staying here."

Tina jumped up from her desk and practically ran around it to stand in front of Colleen.

"What do you want from me?" she asked. "Weeping and wailing?"

"Some feeling would be nice!"

"I'm just going to…" Marco said, getting up and walking out the door.

"I have all the feelings you do," Tina said, her eyes

starting to shine, "but I learned a long time ago that to spill them all didn't do anybody any good! Least of all me!"

"It might've helped me to see you had some!" Colleen said, tears falling fast down her face, stinging the cuts on her cheeks. "To know that you felt something other than cold half the time and rage the other half."

Tina stared at Colleen, her jaw tight. "I can't be anything other than what I am. What *he* made me. If that's not enough for you...well, there's nothing I can do about that."

Colleen's body trembled and she wanted to hug her mother, and be hugged back. She wanted to tell her that it was alright, that she understood, even though she didn't, not really. She had been molded by Grandfather, too, and had chosen to be someone else, though half the time she wasn't sure exactly who that was.

"Now," Tina said, wiping a tear away as if it were a fly on her cheek, "are you gonna sit back down and wait for the doctor, or am I gonna have to tie you down?"

Colleen sat back down, all the fight gone.

Tina stood in front of her for a moment, a brief flash of something like grief crumpling her features, and then it was gone.

"The suit, it fits well?" Tina asked.

"Yes, thank you."

"It looks good on you."

Colleen nodded.

There was a knock on the door, and the doctor came in with his large black bag, Marco trailing him. Colleen drained the rest of the glass and took a deep breath. Marco tried to meet her eye, but Colleen avoided him. Maybe someday she'd try to explain her relationship with her mother, but today wasn't that day.

Maybe when I understand it myself. So then, never I guess.

The doctor got right to work, asking a few questions as he looked both of them over.

236

"I'll start with the you, Miss Knight," the doctor said.

"No, I—"

"The one who bled the most gets my attention first, it's a rule I have. Although," he looked at her arm, white eyebrow cocked, "you cauterized it?"

Colleen felt Tina's eyes intense on her as she nodded.

The doctor stared at her a moment more, expecting an explanation, but Colleen didn't give one.

"Very well," he said. "Let's begin."

As the doctor poked and prodded her arm, Colleen looked over at Tina, who was slumped just a little in her chair, eyes staring distantly at the floor. No matter what had ever happened between the two of them, Colleen and Tina had always had one thing they'd fight to the death to protect, one person that they'd loved no matter what: Andrew. And now he hated them.

Could she do what Tina suggested? Could she put it aside, move on, and not let it haunt her the rest of her life? Would she end up cold like her mother?

It was tempting, to shut it all up somewhere inside and only let it out when she was good and truly drunk. She could move on, live her life without regret or the weight of too much love on her heart.

And I'd be just like her. So, I'll let it live in me. Let it drive me. And one day, I'll see Andrew again. Until then, I'll find out who the hell these people are that think they can cage us and turn us into monsters on a leash.

By the time the doctor was done with both of them, it was past midnight. Tina assured Marco that Liam would be treated with respect, he had only to tell her where the body was to be buried. She ordered a car to take Marco and

Colleen wherever they wanted and asked them to call if they needed anything.

Knowing what he did about Tina, Marco knew he should feel nervous accepting so much help from her. But tonight, he was too tired, too battered inside and out to really care.

The driver pulled up to Allegra's small, brick, cottage-style home and Marco eased himself out, muscles screaming in protest. In the spring, the small front yard was alive with roses, petunias, geraniums and other flowers Marco couldn't name. Now it was barren and dark. A yellow porchlight cast a warm glow in the cold early morning. The small patch of short grass was covered in frost, and the sidewalk slick, as Marco stepped onto it.

"See you tomorrow?" Colleen asked before he closed the door.

"Yeah...where?"

Colleen paused.

"I'll come here," Colleen finally said.

Marco nodded and turned toward the house. Allegra had given him a key when he'd moved back to Metro City, though he'd never used it.

Before he could put the key in the lock, the door opened and Delilah stood there in a blue robe that matched her eyes. She didn't say a word, just grabbed his hand and guided him inside. To his left was a small sitting room filled with pictures, books and old furniture. In front of him, to the right of a long hallway, was a staircase, more framed pictures on the wall that ran along the staircase and up to the second story.

Marco just stood in the entry way, feeling lost and too tired to move. Delilah still held his hand, and after a moment she put her arms around him. There was no seduction or pretense, just sympathy and comfort. He let his head drop into the crook of her neck, his arms going around her soft body, and started to cry.

Minutes passed unnoticed as he poured out everything in his tears, all the loss, the betrayal, the stains on his soul that he knew would never come clean. Delilah held him, tears soaking the neck of her robe. When he finally looked up, she wiped his face with her fingertips and led him upstairs.

He didn't want to be alone with everything that had happened, but he wasn't sure he could use Delilah like that either, so Marco stood in the doorway of a bedroom, unsure. Finally, Delilah tugged him inside and helped him take the bloodied duster and vest off. The moment he slid naked beneath the cool sheets, exhaustion hit him like a truck. He had just enough energy to put his arms around Delilah, his face once again in the crook of her neck, before falling into a deep and dreamless sleep.

CHAPTER TWENTY-ONE

When Marco awoke, late morning sunshine streamed in through the gauzy curtains. The doctor Tina had procured the night before was good, but he could do nothing for the intense aches and pains Marco now suffered. Reaching over to see if Delilah was awake, he instead found the spot empty, except for an envelope on the pillow next to his.

Inside was the key from Dr. Trace and a note.

"Train station, east lockers, number 517. I'm sorry that I hurt you. I'm sorry I wasn't honest. If things had been different, if we'd met like people are supposed to, I wonder what would've happened. But we didn't, so here we are. I will never forget you."

He closed his eyes and sighed, not sure how he had expected things to end with Delilah. And also, not sure if he wanted to know why he felt disappointed that she'd left this way.

After a few minutes he tried to sit up and groaned in pain. He looked down and saw a gruesome patchwork of bruises all over his abdomen and chest. Wincing made his face hurt, so he didn't even want to know how he looked in the harsh light of day.

He walked with the speed and grace of an old man

down the hall and into the bathroom. The reflection that looked back at him in the mirror wasn't as bad as he thought it would be, though it wasn't good either. His right cheek was bruised and cut, his bottom lip was swollen, and his right eye had a deep bruise all around it.

God, I miss Gerald right now…

He ran a hot shower and stepped into the water. It hurt as it fell on his bruised skin, but he ignored the pain, letting the heat soothe his muscles as best it could. After a few minutes, he began to smile as something occurred to him. Then, he began to laugh, but quickly had to stop because it hurt too much.

"I did one thing right," he said to himself. "I got Lionel's cure. At least that much worked out." Ignoring the warning voice in the back of his mind telling him anything could happen, Marco stayed in the shower until the hot water ran out.

He had toweled off and reached toward the closet before he remembered that he didn't have any clothes here. Looking back at the bloodied Shadow suit, Marco frowned, not sure what to do. A knock echoed up to him and he sighed.

Holding tight to the towel wrapped around his waist, he opened the door and smiled at Colleen.

"Hi," she said, large sunglasses hiding her eyes and parts of her cheeks. "Can I come in?"

"Uh…I don't have any clothes."

"Well, it's a good thing I went and picked some up for you, isn't it?"

She held out a garment bag and he took it with a sheepish grin. Before she stepped inside, she grabbed two small white bags off the porch, hissing with pain when she used her right arm.

"How…I mean most of my spare clothes at the gym were probably smoke damaged."

"After months of working with you I know your size. I had Tina's man pick something up for you."

"Thank you for this," he said, wincing from a sudden pain in his side.

"Yeah," Colleen said, removing her sunglasses with a grimace. "I know how you feel."

Both eyes were bruised horribly. The twin cuts on her cheeks were scabbed, but obviously still hurting.

"Apparently my quick healing has it's limits. Where can I take the food?"

"Kitchen's through there, help yourself to whatever is in there. I'll be right back."

Colleen waved him off as she limped toward the kitchen.

Marco had intended to dress in a hurry, but when he moved too quickly, his lower back would seize. So, slow and steady was the only option.

He expected Colleen to be waiting impatiently for him to come downstairs, but when he walked into the kitchen, she was still putting food on plates.

"We're quite the pair," he said, easing onto a kitchen chair across the small table from her.

"Aren't we just?" she said, giving him a painful grin.

He laughed, instantly regretted it, clutching his stomach. Which only made them both laugh.

"So," Colleen said once they'd settled and taken a few sips of coffee, "what now?"

"That's a big question," Marco said. "The only reason you were here was your brother. Now that he's...well, that you know what happened, what does that mean for you?"

Colleen sat back in the chair, brow wrinkled as she took a large drink of steaming coffee.

"I don't know," she finally said. "I liked working with you."

"I liked it, too. You're a good partner."

"Thanks."

"What about that suit?" Marco asked. "Was that a onetime thing?"

"You mean, am I going to be a Metro City vigilante?"

Marco shrugged. "You'd be good at it."

"It did feel good to just let it out, instead of trying to hide it all the time," Colleen said with a grin. Then she shook her head, as if to dislodge the idea. "I'll have to think about it. Tina insisted on repairing the suit, so…"

"You don't want to owe her anything else, is that it?"

Colleen nodded. "What about you?"

"Delilah left me the key. Now, all I have to do is pick up the information."

"And you'll be going back to Jet City."

Marco frowned. "For a little while, yes. But for good? I don't know."

"I suppose," Colleen said, after a few minutes of silence, "we both deserve a little time to figure it all out."

"Yeah, I think we do."

They drank their coffee in silence, each lost in questions and fears they weren't yet ready to share.

A few days later, Marco and Colleen buried Liam in a small plot in the Irish quarter. His grave would be marked with a simple cross with his name and the date of his death, since Marco had no idea when Liam was born. He felt guilty that it took a few days to arrange Liam's funeral, and much longer to coordinate the funeral of the woman who'd condemned Liam to a life of suffering.

He deserved better.

When he attended Allegra's funeral, the day after Christmas, the church of St. Jude's was hot and stuffy with mourners, even as it snowed outside. The smell of perfume, incense and general body odor was amplified by the heat in the church.

At one point, while the priest's deep voice droned the liturgy, Marco found himself drifting off. His Aunt Appolonia simply nudged him and gave him a sad smile, as if excusing his lapse in church etiquette because of his grief.

They all think I'm just overcome with sadness. They don't know...they'll never know.

Emotions collided inside of him as he joined the other pallbearers and carried Allegra's casket to the waiting hearse. Tears fell down his bruised face, yet anger was also there, bright and hot. He hated that he'd never be able to think of her again without feeling betrayed.

Everyone gave him heartfelt sympathies, knowing what Allegra had meant to him, but not having a clue what she'd done or who she'd really been. Marco accepted it all with grace and somber smiles, hiding what he felt until that night, when he sat in Allegra's house, a glass of bourbon in his hand.

Alone, with no one judging, Marco let it all out, stifling his screams of anger in one of the couch pillows.

When Allegra's will was read the next day, Marco discovered that she'd left everything to him. The house, the boxing gym, even her meager savings. It was all his.

Not at all sure he wanted a constant reminder of Allegra, Marco thought about selling the house and gym. He knew, though, that the gym had been a staple of the community since long before he was born, and to take that away just because he wasn't feeling like doing the work didn't seem fair.

The house, however, could go.

Marco hired repairmen to come in and fix the damage to the boxing gym and a month later, he walked through the gym just as the last repairman was fixing some of the lights.

The smell of cheap paint and floor polish stung his eyes, and he hoped the place would air out before it reopened the following week.

Maybe, just maybe, nineteen sixty-two will be different. Maybe it will be a good year.

"There you are," Colleen said, smiling.

The bruises and cuts had healed, though she still favored her arm on occasion. A sad light had taken root in her eyes, especially when she thought Marco wasn't looking. They didn't talk much about Lumis, not even when the papers reported that a government agency had quarantined the area due to poison chemicals.

Marco had gone back once, hiding behind the old barracks to see what was going on. The upper building was as it had been before, but instead of the low parking lot lights from before, the entire place was illuminated with large lights as bright as daylight. Men were moving large boxes from the back of the building to unmarked trucks, their silver and white decontamination suits made them seem alien and strange.

As much as he wanted to know what they were carting out, Marco wasn't stupid enough to get close. He'd seen what the people who worked there thought of people like him. He'd left after about an hour, knowing he wasn't going to get any answers about who was running the place, or where they'd taken the powered people who had been held captive there.

"Did you need something?" Marco asked.

"I wanted to see what you thought about a new PI office around here?"

"So, you're going to be my partner, after all?"

Colleen shrugged. "For the time being. Until something better comes along."

Marco laughed. "Oh, well, thank you for sticking around until then. You have a space in mind?"

"Maybe. There's one here and another in High Tide."

"High Tide?"

Colleen shrugged. "It's not as scary as it used to be."

Marco nodded. "You pick, I trust you."

"Alright then, I'll let you know. I like the new paint color by the way."

The old walls had been a strange light green that always made Marco a little queasy. Now they were a cream color, a nice contrast to the shining wood floors.

"See you for dinner?" Colleen asked before she got to the door.

"You mean you want me to cook?"

"Of course."

Marco smiled. "I'll be at your place at five."

Colleen waved and walked out into the cold clad in her usual warm weather attire.

After checking that the leak in the bathroom had indeed been repaired earlier that day, and that the new towels had been delivered, Marco walked into the back office. He'd managed to clear out half of the boxes that Allegra had kept stacked in the small space, making the room feel spacious by comparison to how it had looked.

Instead of continuing to clear out the small office, Marco went right to the small safe he'd installed, and checked to make sure the files Dr. Trace had left were still there. Seeing that the two file folders were safe, he was about to close the door when he hesitated, and then reached in and took out one of the files.

Though he knew it wouldn't change anything, Marco opened the folder, stared at the top page, and read it for the hundredth time. When he came to the line that had made his stomach lurch the first time he'd read it, Marco stared dragging his eyes word-by-word along the page: "All subjects lose their powered abilities upon taking the cure. No exceptions."

"Nothing can be easy, can it?" he said, replacing the folder and closing the safe.

He had asked Tina if he could see all the files Grandfather had collected about Lumis, hoping it would give him information on how to keep Lionel from losing his powers when he took the cure. But, the more he looked, the more obvious it became that nothing could be done.

He was just closing the safe when the ring of the phone in the office startled him.

"St. Nic's Boxing Gym."

"Marco?" Logan's voice drifted to him from the receiver.

"What's wrong? Is Alice alright?" he asked, his heart clenching.

"She's…Yes, mostly she's fine, but she needs you, Marco. I know you had your reasons for leaving, but…"

"If she needs me, I'll be there."

Logan sighed. "Thank you."

"Do you know if your contacts in Europe have found Lionel?" Marco asked.

"Yes, an old war correspondent friend saw him in Switzerland of all places. He was pretty cagey with the details but he said Lionel got the message."

"Is he there or on his way then?"

"I don't know. We haven't heard anything."

Marco's shoulders slumped.

"He might just want to stay on the run," Logan said.

"Yeah. Well, I'll be on the first plane I can get."

"There's a ticket waiting for you. Tonight at eight."

Marco chuckled.

"Pretty sure of yourself there."

"I'm pretty sure about *you*, Marco."

"See you tonight."

He looked around the hole in wall office and felt at once dread and hope.

Would Alice hate him now? Would Lionel?

Doesn't matter. It's time to finish this. They need me, I'm there.

He took his jacket off the back of the chair and slipped it on. With one last glance at the gym he'd inherited, the life he'd been resigned to building for himself a moment before, Marco turned the lights off and walked out.

ABOUT THE AUTHOR

Trish has been obsessed with stories about female heroes ever since she put on her first pair of Wonder Woman under-roos and spun around. After realizing that fear of failure had been holding her back, Trish became her very own hero and participated in National Novel Writing Month in 2015. Since then, Trish has braved the constant attacks of her nemeses Inner Critic and No Time, in order to achieve the impossible: An artistic life with two small kids!

Trish was one of the co-creators of the super hero comedy web series "The Collectibles". Her first novel "Serpent's Sacrifice" was published in 2017 and is the first book in an Urban Fantasy Superhero series, The Vigilantes.

Trish currently lives in Washington State with her writer/editor/producer husband, and their two geeky daughters.

ACKNOWLEDGMENTS

This was the hardest book to write (I have no idea why!) and so I owe a huge Thank You to my amazing, wonderful husband Dan. You talked me through every doubt, every frustration and helped me to get back to the keyboard. I don't know how many iterations of this story you read or had to listen to me talk about, but you did it all with patience and love. I've said it before and I'll say it to my dying day: I couldn't do this without you.

Thank you to my daughters Rosalind and Cara. You two were there with a funny story or a hug when I needed it, even though you didn't know why I was so sad or upset. You are both my heart, my joy and I love you so much.

To my awesome editor Maria D'Marco, you have taught me so much about how to be a better writer. Your notes and suggestions push me to go deeper and be better. Thank you for all your hard work and encouragement. I feel so lucky to have found you right out of the gate.

My new proofreader is the awesome, the hilarious Raechelle Downing. Thank you for working for such cheap wages (a bottle of whiskey). You smoothing over the things I missed or that came out weird has meant that I'm releasing this book feeling far more confident than I ever have before.

Todd Downing (yep, they're married), your cover for this book was breath taking, and I mean that literally because I actually choked on my water when I saw it. Your work continues to amaze me and make my books look so darn pretty.

To the Advanced Reading Heroes, you all are the best! It means more than you'll ever know that you take the time to read my books and give an honest review. Your emails and Facebook comments encourage me, and the fact that you love The Vigilantes as much as I do makes me so happy! I even have a happy dance that I might show you all some day!

And that brings me to you, the reader of this book. I also couldn't do this without you. Thank you for picking up book three, for reading it and hopefully loving it.

Made in the USA
Middletown, DE
26 September 2019